31192
Starplace, The

THE STARPLACE

THE
STARPLACE

VICKI GROVE

G. P. PUTNAM'S SONS ★ NEW YORK

ACKNOWLEDGMENTS

I would like to thank Evelyn Pulliam, who graciously read this manuscript from a perspective I could only try to imagine, but could never know from the inside out.

I would also like to thank the family in our town who found a shocking document beneath the floorboards of their attic and agreed to share it with me. Much of the terminology and description of ritual in Chapter 22 was gleaned from this secret rule book, and the fact that my friends wish to remain anonymous after sharing this information speaks of deeply rooted dangers still present in our society.

Finally, and as always, I'm extremely grateful to my perceptive and patient editor, Anne O'Connell.

a division of Penguin Putnam Books for Young Readers,
345 Hudson Street, New York, NY 10014.
G. P. Putnam's Sons, Reg. U.S. Pat. & Tm. Off.
Published simultaneously in Canada. Printed in the United States of America.
Designed by Gunta Alexander. Text set in Garamond #3.
Library of Congress Cataloging-in-Publication Data
Grove, Vicki. The starplace / by Vicki Grove.   p.   cm.
Summary: Thirteen-year-old Frannie learns hard lessons about prejudice and segregation when she becomes friends with a young black girl who moves into her small Oklahoma town in 1961. [1. Segregation—Fiction.
2. Prejudices—Fiction. 3. Afro-Americans—Fiction. 4. Oklahoma—Fiction.]
I. Title. PZ7.G9275St 1999 [Fic]—dc21   98—40894   CIP   AC
ISBN 0-399-23207-9   10 9 8 7 6 5 4 3 2 1   First Impression

For Mary Alice Grove,
from one of her biggest fans

CHAPTER 1

I saw Celeste for the first time on the last day of August, 1961.

It was hot and steamy, like nearly every August Saturday is in Oklahoma. Margot, Nancy, Kelly and I had been hanging around my patio most of the afternoon, all of us in our swimsuits, except Kelly. She had on cut-off jeans and her dark red cowgirl boots because she was riding Nibbles, who kept eagerly munching the clump of still-green grass that grew beneath where our leaky garden hose connected to the house.

Margot and Nancy were sitting knee-to-knee in the tiny strip of shade the redwood fence was giving the patio. They'd been trying for hours to plan a back-to-school party, but they couldn't get past arguing about what the theme should be.

"Fran-*nie,* mon cheri, it's *your* patio," Margot suddenly yelled across to me, jumping to her feet and throwing up her short, white arms. "Tell her it has to be 'Evening in Paris'!"

Margot is one-eighth French. She spent all of our seventh grade year trying to get everyone to spell her name the French way—Margeaux.

"No, it simply *must* be 'Hawaiian Luau'!" Nancy corrected in this too-patient voice that sounded like somebody's long-suffering mother. She swung her legs to the side, pushed up onto her knees, then sort of staggered the rest of the way to her feet. This was the ladylike way of getting up from the ground, she was always telling us, but it seemed to me like the way really *old* ladies would do it.

"You *know* you agree with *me*, Frannie," she informed me when she was finally standing, brushing daintily at the tiny pieces of concrete gravel that studded her dimply white thighs. I noticed little red pressure marks in the centers of her knees.

It was too hot. I pretended I hadn't heard either of them and went right on doing what I was doing, which was roller skating. I'd just gotten fancy white shoe skates for my thirteenth birthday, three weeks before. They were tons faster and smoother than my old clamp-on metal skates, and the television announcer for the 1960 winter Olympics was raving about how good I'd suddenly gotten.

Francine Driscoll, Olympic medalist and Worldwide Queen of the Rink, skates a victory lap to receive roses from the adoring crowd! And LOOK AT THAT, sports fans! Un-be-liev-able! She's skating it . . . yes, she's actually skating it BACKWARDS!

"Frannie, decide!" Margot yelled, flipping her head in that way French girls in movies flip their heads to swish around their tons of shiny French hair. Margot was always flipping, flipping, flipping, but it never even phased her short, tight permanent. "If this party flops, you'll be the one people will blame, you know, since it's going to be on *your* patio! C'est la vie, c'est la vou, mamselle la party la stinke*roo!*"

"No one believes that's actual French, Margot," Nancy informed her with a big, flouncy sigh. "And Frannie can't hear you anyway. She's pretending some sports announcer is saying what a great skater she is."

Flustered, I stuck a toe brake down to the concrete so fast I nearly lost my balance. "You guys said you'd take the blame if this was a disaster. In fact, if you're not going to take the blame, then I think we'd better just reconsider the whole—"

"Now look what you've done, Margot!" Nancy scolded, wagging one sharp, no-nonsense fingernail at her. "You know Frannie can't stand to be blamed for *any*thing."

Huh? Was that true?

3

"A luau," Kelly suddenly drawled from up on Nibbles. "You can't get Oklahoma to be Paris, but you could get it to be Hawaii a little bit. We got these mimosa trees. And we got this green fence. Where the paint's peeling looks like tropical leaves."

We all looked at the tall fence which edged the square little patio on two sides. We looked at the four mimosa trees with their glaring pink blossoms, then at the fence again.

Kelly was so right that even Margot couldn't deny it, at least not in English. But she rolled her eyes and pressed her hands to the sides of her face. "Je ma oui! Le luau? Horriblay idea! Horri*blay!*"

Nancy smiled sweetly like she always did when she got her way, then straightened her shoulders and crossed her arms. She was even more pear-shaped than usual when she stood with her heels together and her toes pointing slightly outward like that, but I knew she thought she looked elegant. She was probably trying to teach us by example the gracious, ladylike way to accept victory once you'd worn your opponent to a frazzle.

"Now, we'll need positively *acres* of crepe paper, in green and all sorts of bright colors," she instructed. "I see torches and palm trees and bunches and bunches of flower leis. School starts Monday, and we'll put invitations in all the eighth grade lockers Thursday and have the luau Friday night."

She nailed me with her don't-even-*think*-about-ignoring-me expression before I could skate away.

The crowd chants for Francine's return, but the overwhelming demands of her public force her early departure from the rink. Word is, sports fans, she's been tagged to take the blame for some sort of doomed enterprise involving crepe paper. Stay tuned.

"Before we start, we better get dressed and go clear this with my mom." I sighed, stooping to untie my laces.

"Her office is *miles* from here," Margot groaned. "Too hot!"

No one had the gumption to correct her. It *was* a long eight blocks away.

"We'll cut through the field," Kelly said.

Her suggestion was greeted with stupified silence.

"Actually walk . . . through it?" Nancy finally asked, her voice small for once.

Kelly shrugged. "I cut through all the time," she said.

But that was Kelly, whose cowgirl nature made her charge ahead with things other people might think were crazy. While she tethered Nibbles to our clothesline, Nancy, Margot and I spent several minutes that hot afternoon just standing in the sticky, tarry alley that ran behind my subdivision in Quiver, Oklahoma, facing the field and trying to get up our nerve. My mother's office was located on Route 66, three treacherous blocks straight ahead if you dared to use this shortcut, which I hardly ever did. From where we were standing, we couldn't quite see the strip of businesses where her office was, but we could see the highway's endless parade of toy-sized cars, shimmering in the heat.

I knew Margot and Nancy just dreaded slogging through the waist-high rye grass and thorny weeds, but the field seemed sort of *weird* to me. Off. Not quite right. Several things had been built in it over the years, but nothing had lasted. Everything anyone had attempted in the field had either fallen to pieces, been taken apart and moved someplace else, or burned down. A tractor dealership was built out there, but went quickly out of business, then just stood disintegrating until the town bulldozed it. The same thing happened with the hamburger place built out there next. The thing that burned down was a car parts store. When that mess was cleaned up, Quiver had tried building a playground. Swing bars were put up, and a thirty-foot-tall rocket ship was set in concrete, with a slide in its belly. But at the last minute, everyone decided that a field edging busy Route 66 was the most horrible place in the world for a playground.

The swing bars and sandbox were moved, but the rocket ship couldn't be budged from its concrete pad. It was left to point forever straight up from the field like

God's forefinger. Sometimes at night, when I was looking out my bedroom window at the moving lights that were Route 66, the dark, silhouetted field would seem to me like a huge, mangy animal with that one splinter of rust that was the rocket ship sticking straight up from its rump and making it grouchy enough to devour anything—or any*one*—who crossed its path.

"Okay, let's do it," Kelly ordered.

I shivered my late-night imaginings away, which wasn't that hard in this bright sunshine, and as Nibbles watched us from her nice, safe position tethered to the clothesline, we began working our way across the field, thrashing along as thorns ripped into our arms and bare legs and insects flew into our noses and open, panting mouths.

When we finally stumbled out on the other side, we were soaked with sweat, our hair and socks were filled with cockleburrs, and we were totally nerve-wracked and miserable.

"Sacre *bleu!* I'm never—I repeat, *never!*—going in there again!" Margot whimpered. Tight curls clung to her red forehead as we traipsed the last easy block from the field to the realty office.

I glanced over at Kelly. Her straight, yellow-white hair was as tangled and buggy as any of ours, but she wasn't rubbing and fanning and scratching like we were. She was just walking straight ahead in that arm-swinging cowgirl way of hers, not paying attention to either her own discomfort or our constant moaning.

Then suddenly, she stopped. "Who's that?" she asked.

I shielded my eyes with one hand and squinted at the large, shiny black car that was idling in one of the customer slots at the realtors. No one in Quiver drove anything like that. The closest thing would have been the limousine owned by the funeral home.

"Someone looking at houses, I guess," I answered uncertainly, trying to knot my sweat-sopped hair into some kind of braid.

The car's tinted windows were rolled up. We walked closer, and on an impulse I ran over and cupped my hands into a viewing tunnel on the front right window. I looked over my shoulder, checking to be sure the customer was still in the office before I bent to take a quick look inside. Did cars like this have television sets and fold-out bars with martini glasses?

"Fran-*nie!* That's private property!" Nancy scolded in a whisper.

Mostly to disobey Nancy, I pressed my forehead harder against my cupped hands, and when my eyes adjusted to the cool dimness inside the car, I saw a girl who turned out to be Celeste, sitting quietly as a shadow in the right front passenger seat, staring directly back at me.

CHAPTER 2

I slapped both hands together, keeping the edges of my palms firmly against the window and leaving two smeary sweat trails behind on the glass.

"Don't worry, I think I got it!" I yelled to the unmoving girl on the other side of the glass. My heart was slamming. "Dragonbee—a big one, too! Could have been deadly, but I . . . uh, got it. Don't worry!"

Stiff-arming my hands far in front of me, grimacing as though my poor palms were being stung to pieces, I ran to the edge of the parking lot where I fake-dropped something small but horrible into the grass and thoroughly annihilated it with the toe of my right tennis shoe.

I waved elaborately toward the girl in the car—*no need to thank me, just doing my duty as a good citizen*—and ducked on into the small entrance lobby of my mom's building, my whole body burning.

Seconds later, my friends clattered in right behind me, giggling their heads off. "Sacre *bleu!*" Margot squealed.

"I'll *kill* anyone who says another word—got that?" I informed them.

"Did you act like that because she was colored?" Margot whispered in a rush.

"What?"

"Is that why you acted so weird, because the girl in that car was a Negro," Kelly explained. "It's not like we see one downtown every day."

I just looked at them. "I *did* that because there was a dangerous insect just *waiting* to get a chance to *sting* her!"

Nancy stepped forward then and put her hand on the doorknob into the main office. "The luau, remember?" she said, shaking her head and sighing.

We must have looked pretty scruffy, dragging toward my mother's reception desk that day. She put a finger quickly to her lips as we tiptoed in and sat quietly in the line of folding chairs along the wall beside her desk.

"Mr. Joslen's with a client," she mouthed, gesturing with her shoulder toward the biggest of the three inner office rooms.

Mr. Joslen's door was open, and his laughing voice kept booming out of it. I could see his big feet crossed in their shiny shoes on top of some of the papers that cluttered the corner of his desk. I could also see the gray material covering the right knee of the client, with one of his chocolate-colored hands resting lightly on it.

"Well, Raymond, I'd sure be very pleased to show you some of these nice properties," Mr. Joslen boomed out, so loud you had to hear. "Raymond, as I say, Foxgrape Woods is just entirely filled at this time, and there's quite a little waiting list for the future expansion out there. But there's some other fine and dandy places I could show you that are available for immediate occupancy. Whattayasay? Come on, boy, let's go *do* her."

The springs of his swivel chair squealed, and Mr. Joslen came out of his office, hiking up his pants. The other man walked out just in front of him, holding a gray hat in both hands. You could see beefy Mr. Joslen all the way around the slender client.

They stopped in front of my mother's desk. Mr. Joslen put one of his hands on the other man's shoulder and said to my mother, "Caroline, this here is Raymond Chisholm, a newcomer to our fair city. Raymond, this here is Mrs. Caroline Driscoll, the sweetest little woman anybody ever had working for them." He turned partly away and fake-whispered loudly to the man, "And she's easy on the eyes, too."

Mr. Joslen laughed and winked, and my mother blushed.

The client slowly held his long-fingered hand out to

11

my mother. His nails were smooth-edged and shiny. "Mrs. Driscoll, pleased to make your acquaintance," he said. Then he turned to Mr. Joslen. "If you don't mind, Mr. Joslen, I generally go by Mr. Chisholm rather than 'Raymond' or 'boy' when I'm transacting business."

Things got quiet.

"Greatgreatgreat!" Mr. Joslen finally boomed, taking his hand carefully off Mr. Chisholm's shoulder. "Whatever the client wants, right Caroline? Now, we'll be back later on, so you just hold down the fort, pretty lady."

Again he winked broadly at my mother, turned to playfully point a finger-gun at the four of us, then held the door politely open for Mr. Chisholm to follow.

Mr. Chisholm didn't follow him immediately, though. He walked over to stand in front of our line of folding chairs and bent slightly to get closer to our level. "I believe you girls may be about the age of my daughter, Celeste," he said softly. Then he smiled at us, maybe waiting for one of us to speak.

We didn't, though. We all just sat there, gawking. No one in Quiver wore suits in August, or suits anytime that looked as elegant as his. And I somehow knew that the tiny spark of light in his tietack was a real diamond. Anyone in Quiver would have chosen a big, huge rhinestone thinking no one would know the difference.

He smiled at us again, then raised his hat almost to his head and nodded to my mother, who smiled and nodded back. Then he walked past Mr. Joslen, who was running his fingers around in the pockets of his pants and bouncing on his heels impatiently.

My mother still seemed flustered after the door whooshed closed behind them. "What *manners,*" she breathed, and she seemed to be barely listening as we told her our luau plans. "Yes, yes, that's fine," she said, then fumbled in her purse and gave us money to get Cokes and fries at Skif's Drugstore down the block. She told us she'd pick us up there and drive us home when she got off.

I planned to give the girl—Celeste—another elaborate wave when we passed her again, but the black car was gone when we got back outside.

In roughly the place it had been parked, Max, Jason and Theodore C. Rockman were doing figure eights in the three-seater go-cart they'd built from scratch in Jason's garage early in the summer.

Max was driving, wearing this long red scarf around his neck he always wore when he was behind the wheel. Jason was sitting next to him with his binoculars up to his eyes, and Theodore C. Rockman was balanced in the little basket of a side-seat that stuck out like a hornet's nest. His briefcase was smashed in beside him, and he had his hairy knees tucked up to his chin.

"Beware, you blackguards!" Max yelled above the

popping racket of the motor. He shook his fist at some bored-looking bluejays that were perched on the JOSLEN REALTY sign. "You can fly from us, but you can't hide! We'll be back for you!"

Max, Jason and Theodore were playing their favorite game, chasing birds. Everyone had been horrified when they first started that game, but now it was obvious they would never even come close to running over a bird in a million years. It was also obvious they didn't want to—I'd caught Max braking for the one silly sparrow I'd ever seen accidentally wind up in their way.

We waved, and Jason trained the binoculars on us. "Get the big corner booth at Skif's!" he yelled, and we nodded to tell them we understood.

"What about them and the party?" Kelly asked as we walked on to Skif's.

I shrugged. "Nancy says we're inviting everyone in eighth grade, remember? Besides, they *are* some of our best friends."

"Just not the kind you're crazy about having in the way when there are *real* boys in the vicinity," Margot said, which was roughly what we were all thinking. "We need to drop them this year. They are just *so* immature."

We heard the putter of the go-cart pulling out of its curve and coming up slowly behind us.

"We could at least tell them they can't bring the go-cart or their briefcases to the luau," Nancy suggested.

"And they've got to act normal, not . . . smart. They can't suddenly get out their calculators or a chess board or a copy of *Time Magazine* or anything. They've *got* to be normal, or everyone will leave. *Tell* them that, Frannie!"

"Why *me?*"

"Because, mon cheri, the party's on *your* patio and everyone will blame you if it doesn't go right!" Margot reminded me, again.

CHAPTER 3

Nancy was right about me, I decided. I couldn't stand the thought of "my" party being humiliating, but I couldn't stand the thought of telling Max, Theodore and Jason that they had to be normal, either. I couldn't stand to be blamed for *any*thing. But that was sort of a good trait, wasn't it? It just meant you were careful and conscientious.

Tell them! Nancy mouthed the words across to me as we all sat in Skif's big round corner booth, slurping cherry-vanilla Cokes and sharing fries.

I widened my eyes and twitched my head back and forth one tiny time—*no!* When we gave out the invitations we could tell them, maybe in a footnote. *P.S. No intelligent behavior, please. Act brainless like everybody else or you'll be asked to leave.*

"Tell us what?" Jason asked, giving me his usual gentle, unsuspecting smile. He had ketchup all over his long, pointed front teeth.

I shot Nancy a subtle dirty look, then turned back to Jason. "Tell you . . . that we just had something interesting happen at my mom's office. This Negro man came in looking for property in Foxgrape Woods. Nothing's available out there, but Mr. Joslen is taking him to look at other places. In Minetown, I guess."

If Quiver had been a little bigger than fifteen thousand people, you might have called Minetown a suburb. It was where the zinc mines were, where Quiver began to trickle away into dusty plains and scrub brush. It wasn't a town exactly, just the far edge of Quiver. All the black people lived in Minetown.

Theodore C. Rockman sat up very straight and frowned at something in the distance. With his long, greased-back dark hair and thick, goggle-shaped glasses, Theodore always looked a lot like an otter sniffing the air when he did that.

"There are several houses for sale in Foxgrape Woods," he said, taking off his glasses and smoothing the adhesive tape that held them together in the middle. "The man was obviously told there was nothing available because that area is strictly restricted."

" 'Strictly restricted' is a possible redundancy," Max mentioned.

"Conceded," Theodore said, giving him a nod. "I should merely have said 'restricted.'"

"Restricted?" I'd only heard the word used by my grandmother. She was always squeezing into her girdle, then complaining that the blood flow to her legs was restricted.

"That means no colored people are allowed to live out there," Max said, touching each side of his mouth with a napkin. At some point, he'd wrapped his long red scarf several times around his head, making a sort of turban. "No Negroes, and probably no dark-skinned Indians like Theodore, for that matter."

Theodore looked at him. "Maximillian, you yourself being nearly full-blooded Quapaw might very well qualify for exclusion more than I, at one-half Cherokee."

Lots of the kids in our Oklahoma town were part Indian, but I'd never thought about some being more dark-skinned than others. I always just thought Theodore, for instance, tanned easily, which seemed like a waste on somebody as unfashion conscious as he was.

"Nearly full-blooded is non-specific and leads to ambiguity," Jason stated. "One would either be full-blooded or not be."

"Conceded," Max and Theodore said together.

"Do they allow horses?" Kelly asked.

Jason nodded. "Oh, sure, there are lots of horses out there. Lots of dogs, too. Fancy ones. In winter, they dress them in sweaters. The poodles wear rhinestone necklaces."

That struck us funny. Margot, for all her great Frenchness and maturity, got Coke up her nose, giggling and drinking at once, and her sputtering struck us funny, too. Then Max stuck two fries under his upper lip like tusks, and all of us slouched in our seats, rocking with laughter. Except for Theodore C. Rockman, who sat up straight and dignified, looking more than ever like an otter, surrounded at the moment by other wildlife too foolish for him to acknowledge—say, frogs.

Earlier in the summer I'd decided I was wasting too much time thinking. I had to cut down if I was going to have the concentration for important eighth grade things, like keeping track of the latest hairstyles and throwing big, splashy patio parties.

So I'd developed a system. Now I saved up all my thinking and did it while I spied on my next-door neighbor Charlotte out my bedroom window late each night.

Charlotte, who was going to be a senior, had a boyfriend with a purple '56 Chevy. It was a loud car, a muscle car, but Charlotte's boyfriend Jay just idled it along when he came skulking into our alley, then shut off the engine several houses up and coasted to a stop behind the trash cans, which were really more behind our house than hers.

That night, as I waited with my chin in my hands and my elbows on my windowsill for the rumble of Jay's Chevy, I started thinking about that restricted stuff Theodore had told us about. Wouldn't being told where they could or couldn't live make people mad? It must have, or Mr. Joslen wouldn't have thought he had to lie to Mr. Chisholm about Foxgrape Woods.

Mr. Chisholm's daughter's face drifted into my mind, the perfectly still way she'd watched me as I bent to peer into her window. She'd seemed so . . . absorbed. Once when I was walking past the hippo pool at the Oklahoma City Zoo, out of nowhere a hippo thrust up from the water and opened her huge, rubbery-white mouth just inches from me. *That* had been absorbing, in an ugly, shocking way.

Had I seemed like that hippo to Mr. Chisholm's daughter, Celeste?

I was so deep in thought I didn't even realize Jay had coasted up, until suddenly Charlotte came running stealthily through the dead grass of her yard, then climbed over her chainlink fence with her full skirt blowing and snagging and her Windsong perfume so strong you could smell it clear over in our yard, even through the too-sweet smell of the mimosa blossoms.

As usual, Jay got slowly from his car. He stood there in the alley shadows and slung his weight back on one hip as he turned up the collar of his black leather jacket.

I saw the spark as he threw his cigarette away. I grabbed my pillow and hugged it as Charlotte and Jay embraced right there in the bug-swarm under the pole light.

Oh my love, my love! Hold me! Kiss me!

I could hardly breathe, because unknown to anyone in the entire universe, I myself was having an intense romance with Robin the Boy Wonder, sidekick of Batman. I'd run across him in one of my cousin's comic books early in the summer. Both Jay and Robin had strong, strong arms and hair so shiny and black it looked painted on. Both were the dangerous, passionate type.

Frenzied with love, Robin once again steals the Batmobile so that he can sneak through the streets of Gotham City to crush beautiful young Francina against his strong, muscular chest, and whisper into her hair that . . .

Charlotte's father suddenly turned on the back porch light. "Charlotte you get yourself into this house this minute or you'll wisht you had!"

I froze, groaned silently, and covered my face with the pillow.

It was so awful when Charlotte got caught like this!

Jay jumped back into his Chevy and peeled away, leaving poor Charlotte to scramble clumsily over the fence and slink miserably through her yard to face the music alone. Even her perfume smelled different—sort of like rotten bananas.

She was barely back inside her house when another

car pulled slowly into our alley that night. For one awful minute I thought it was a police car—a couple of times Charlotte's father had threatened to call the cops on Jay.

And then it rolled into the soupy halo of bugs around the pole light, and I recognized the shiny black car from the realtor's office this afternoon! Mr. Chisholm stopped the car just past Charlotte's house, and he and his daughter both got out.

Why hadn't they stopped under the pole light? I could barely see them from here! I leaned forward so far my left cheek was plastered against the screen of the window.

Two lines of white suddenly appeared in the black sky—Mr. Chisholm and his daughter had flashlights and they were moving into . . . the *field?* What were they looking for? What were they up to? What if they were doing something awful out in the field because they were mad at all of us here in Quiver?

I ran into the living room.

My dad's show was on—*Dragnet.* They were playing the sinister background music that meant Sergeant Joe Friday was about to pick up on another clue—*Dum-duh-Dum-Dum. Dum-duh-Dum-Dum-DUHHH!*

"Mom, was that man, that Mr. Chisholm, angry about being called 'boy' when he left your office this afternoon?" I asked in a rush.

"Who's angry?" Daddy asked without taking his eyes from the screen.

"No one's angry," Mom explained. "She's referring to this colored gentleman who came in today looking for property in Foxgrape Woods." She put her hand on her throat and added dreamily, "He had the most gorgeous manners."

"But Foxgrape Woods is restricted so he couldn't get a house there," I said, mostly to show off. "Did *that* make him angry, Mom?"

The commercial came on and Daddy leaned forward to turn the volume down and said to Mom, "He got angry?"

"No, Sam. No one was angry. He seemed quite pleasant, and Dirk Joslen took him around and actually sold him a house this afternoon."

"A house in Minetown?" I asked.

Before she could answer, Daddy murmured, "Wouldn't we *all* like some property in Foxgrape Woods. I sure couldn't afford to live out there and you don't see me getting angry about it."

Mom faced him till she was sure he was through, then turned to me. "Mr. Joslen intended to show him a number of nice houses, Frannie, but apparently when they drove by the old Teschler place, Mr. Chisholm saw it was vacant and asked if it was for sale and insisted on buying it on the spot."

"Hmmm." Daddy sounded surprised, but a different kind of surprised than I was. "Sold him a house right here in Quiver. *That's* a first." Frowning, he leaned forward to turn the volume up again, with the Pepsodent toothpaste tubes still dancing around.

"The old haunted house?" I asked eagerly. "Why'd he want *that?*"

Mom put a finger to her lips, then whispered, "Frannie, just because the Jaycees used the Teschler house as a spook house for you kids last Hallowe'en doesn't mean it's haunted."

Which, of course, I knew perfectly well. But I also knew that house had been picked for our spook house because it *seemed* haunted to everybody. The Teschler house had the same kind of creepy, not-right feeling to it that the field did.

"That strange old place seems a poor choice," Daddy murmured.

I waited for more, but when he settled back in his chair and didn't go on, I whispered to Mom, "Did you meet Mr. Chisholm's daughter Celeste? Did she act like *she* was angry?"

"I didn't meet her, hon. Now let your poor dad watch his show," Mom said.

Mr. Chisholm and his daughter Celeste were still roaming around in the field with those flashlights when

I got back to my room. I settled in again with my elbows on the windowsill, wishing I had Jason's binoculars. I decided not to worry about the Chisholms being angry, since that could have been a motive, but I couldn't think of a crime they could be about to do. Yes, a motive, but no crime. No answer to this mystery . . . yet.

My name is Driscoll. F.E. Driscoll, girl detective. My friends call me Frannie, and the criminals hope they never have to call me anything at all. The public can sleep a little sounder tonight because F.E. Driscoll is alert in the darkness, pursuing every angle, sifting every lead, every shred of evidence. Oh, yes, Driscoll will get to the bottom of this mystery of the searchers from the spook house no matter how many hours of secret surveillance it takes. Dum-duh-Dum-Dum-DUHHHH!

CHAPTER 4

Theodore C. Rockman and Nancy went to my church. The three of us usually sat together on the back pew, where all the kids our age sat. That next morning the preacher droned on and on about a wall that had just suddenly been built in a faraway city called Berlin, but Nancy and I had more important things on our minds— namely, the luau. I was also still thinking about the Chisholms and what I'd seen in the field last night, but I didn't want to discuss my secret surveillance with anyone yet, for security reasons.

I don't have a bunch of that stuff we need, I wrote on the back on an offering envelope, then handed it to Theodore to hand to Nancy.

Like what? she wrote back.

I took another envelope. *Crepe paper, and my mother doesn't want us using up all her tape. Anyhow, I don't get how we make these palm trees. And won't the boys burn the house down with torches? My mom wants to know.*

Nancy read my note, but before she could answer it, Theodore snatched his briefcase up from the floor and put it on his lap for a writing surface. He grabbed my note from Nancy and added his own note under it, pressing down with one of the many stubby pencils he kept in his shirt pocket.

Theodore's part of the note read: *Don't the two of you care one iota about the fate of democracy and the entire free world?*

I chewed my lip, thinking. *I guess we could use construction paper for the torches, and put flashlights inside* I finally wrote back to Nancy.

We got to work decorating my patio that afternoon. It turned out Nancy knew all about making papier mâché—she'd been her mother's assistant doing some project with her little sister's Brownie troop where they'd made a million papier mâché animals. Nancy was always being some grown-up's assistant.

"Guess what, you guys," I told them. "That girl we saw in the black limo and her father? Well, they bought the old Teschler place."

Everybody stopped what they were doing and looked at me like *I* was the crazy person who'd just bought a rundown old spook house.

27

"With a car like that, why wouldn't they buy something good?" Kelly asked.

"Her father will have to use that limo to drive her miles to school and back every single day," Nancy said. "The buses from Minetown don't run to Quiver to pick kids up for Carver Junior High. I wonder if he knows that."

"Maybe she plans to go to Quiver Junior," Kelly said.

"She couldn't, could she?" Margot asked. "It wouldn't be . . . legal and stuff. Our school is like Foxgrape Woods. What's that word Theodore used? Restricted. Quiver Junior High is restricted to white kids, isn't it?"

She looked at me, but I just shrugged. I could sort of remember there being stuff about Negroes and schools in our seventh grade social studies book, but the teacher skipped over that section because none of us were Negro so we didn't need to know it.

"Nibbles, no!" Nancy suddenly screamed. "Bad horse, bad *horse!*"

Nibbles was drinking out of the bucket we had clean water in to mix with our paste.

"Now it's *germy,*" Nancy complained, wringing her hands, which couldn't have been easy since she was wearing big yellow rubber kitchen gloves.

Margot and I jerked our heads toward Kelly. You never, ever criticized her horse.

"For your information, horses have cleaner mouths than humans," Kelly said calmly without looking up from the piece of chicken wire she was wrestling into the shape of a palm-tree trunk. "Scientific research has proven it. *Your* mouth's the one that's germy."

Uh-oh. Margot and I both held our breath as Kelly stood, put her hands on her hips, threw one long leg over the chicken wire tangle and stepped across it to face Nancy. Nancy lifted her chin, pulled off her gloves with a rubbery snap, crossed her arms so the freckled fat above her elbows bulged almost like muscles, and faced Kelly right back.

They were like two old-time gunfighters, each waiting for the other to make a move—Nancy with her round shoulders, wearing the kind of flowered triangle scarf over her short blonde hair your mother wore to protect her hairstyle when she cleaned out the oven, and Kelly, all points and angles with her cowgirl hat hanging across her shoulder blades, dangling from a sweat-stained string around her neck. Nancy was always so sure her opinions on everything were *absolutely* right, and Kelly never seemed to give anyone's opinions a thought one way or the other, unless they were about her horse. *Then,* watch out.

I looked over at Margot, but I had to look quickly away because her hairy legs seemed gorilla-like when the sun was this bright. The rest of our class had started shaving around a year ago, but Margot thought body hair looked French.

"Kelly, you should go to church," Nancy finally said, lifting her quivering chin. "Sometimes . . . sometimes you don't sound very Christian."

"She didn't mean that you *personally* have a germy mouth, Nancy," I tried to explain.

But the afternoon was pretty much spoiled. Eventually Kelly gave a quick sigh of frustration, then turned and knelt to keep working on that piece of chicken wire. Nancy sniffed her tears back loudly and dramatically, then put on her gloves and got back to work too. But everybody was tense like they always were when Kelly and Nancy collided head-on.

I found myself wishing I could just get them all to leave so I could spend this last day of freedom before school started skating with my secret love, Robin.

May I have this dance, er, I mean, this skate, Francina? Let me put my muscular arm around your waist and we'll just twirl and twirl endlessly on this almost-Hawaiian patio, even skating backwards part of the time to the cheers of your many adoring fans.

But they didn't go home until my mother called me in for dinner.

A few days before, my parents had moved the television set into the space that separated the dining room and living room, so the TV could be faced in either direction. I thought they'd done it so my five-year-old twin brothers, Harley and Mitch, wouldn't always be sneaking their dessert into the living room to watch TV.

It turned out, though, that they'd moved it so they wouldn't miss any of the news, which Walter Cronkite kept calling "fast-breaking."

"Let's go to Roger on location in Berlin," Walter Cronkite said, like he'd been doing every night. A newsguy in Berlin came on. Far behind him you could see a bunch of tangled barbed wire and some guys with machine guns.

As I reluctantly put a piece of liver on my plate, the newsman said, "The Wall was constructed with great speed from prefabricated blocks of concrete, and is already proving to be a highly effective way of stopping the tide of East Germans who have rejected their totalitarian government and fled to the democratic West. East German soldiers, armed with machine guns, now make crossings impossible, as the Wall slices through the very heart of Berlin . . . "

"Big deal," I mentioned. "It's clear on the other side of the ocean from here."

"Big deal," Mitch echoed, trying to stick a slice of bacon into Harley's ear.

My dad usually liked to just eat and not talk, but he surprised me by saying, "It *is* a big deal, Frannie. How would you like it if we all lived in North Dakota and Aunt Celia and her family lived in South Dakota, and suddenly armed guards said they'd shoot us dead if we tried to cross the border into South Dakota to visit all of them at Christmas?"

I thought about pointing out that my snotty cousins drove me crazy, especially at Christmas, when they all ate candy non-stop and were hyperactive. But of course I just lied and said, "I guess I wouldn't like it."

I chewed my liver for a while, thinking. "So, this West Berlin is the same as Foxgrape Woods, right? You can't live there unless the big shots in charge of things say you can."

Neither of my parents answered me at first. Then Daddy said, "Fran, there's a big difference between having your freedom taken away at gunpoint by Communists and being able to live in a luxury home in a restricted area because you've worked hard and taken advantage of the opportunities within our democratic system to be able to afford it."

"Yeah, but see, Mr. Chisholm *can* afford it," I pointed out. "So wouldn't that make him like the guys who can't live in West Berlin and wouldn't that make the big shots at Foxgrape Woods like the Communists, kind of?"

Dad cleared his throat and looked at the TV. "Let's just finish our dinner," he said in this gravelly voice.

Mom was cutting Mitch's meat in this fast, jagged way that told me she was shocked at me, too.

To tell the truth, I'd even shocked myself, comparing Americans to Communists like that. Questioning the news was only a game I'd developed to take my mind off liver and beets and a couple of other kinds of food, but I'd gotten carried away tonight and suddenly called Americans . . . *Communists,* a word so evil you could hardly say it out loud.

My face was burning and I felt even more nauseous than I usually did when we had liver. "Excuse me," I mumbled, and escaped outside to the patio. A tiny hot breeze was stirring the mimosa branches, making them hiss like even *they* were disappointed in me.

CHAPTER 5

In a haze of self-disgust, I maneuvered around the half-finished papier mâché palms and wandered sadly out to the backyard. It wouldn't be truly dark for an hour or so, but across the field on Route 66 some of the cars had their headlights on.

Where were all those people going? Where had they all been?

I leaned against a mimosa tree and felt its rough bark chew into my backbone. Who was I to question anything my parents told me? They *always* knew who the good guys and the bad guys were! And of course the guys who owned Foxgrape Woods were the good guys or they wouldn't be so rich, which was how things worked in a democracy. How unpatriotic could I get?

Being blamed for anything was awful, but of all the

things you could be blamed for, being unpatriotic was probably the very worst.

"You're horrible, Frannie! Just stupid and horrible!" I informed myself. My throat felt tight and throbby. "Wise up," I added in a rough whisper. "You're a teenager now, remember? You're a . . . *woman.*"

One more summer was officially over tonight. One more summer that I hadn't gotten a great tan, or found my perfect hairstyle, or figured out my face shape, which *Seventeen Magazine* said was the key to creating your own unique look with the subtle use of contour make-up.

Then, before I knew what was happening, I was running over the hard dry grass of the backyard, then over the sticky asphalt of the alley.

I hesitated there, expecting to be too scared to go farther, but I was too upset by real life that night for my imagination to dredge up much of my usual fear of the field. In fact, the field's blowing wildness suddenly appealed to me as much as it scared me. I wanted to be swallowed up by it. I *wanted* to be hidden in its mysterious tangle. *Daring young Fran E. Driscoll stands on the very edge of the known world!*

My heart raced, and the wind blew my hair straight back from my face.

"I'm coming, Robin!" I called, and began running clumsily but urgently into the field.

Then, before I knew what was happening, I was veering toward the rocket ship.

I'd never considered going up into the rocket before. But that last night of my thirteenth summer, with my self-disgust and the Berlin Wall and confusingly restricted stuff all tangling in my head, I think I suddenly saw it was a way to get above things.

The slide had long since been taken out of the rocket, but there was a ladder with twelve metal rungs leading from the ground to the wide circular stand where it had once been. As I climbed, I expected the ladder to sway a little, but it didn't. Feeling like I was in a dream, I pulled myself up onto the splintery slide stand and saw the bars which bent to form the top of the rocket coming to a gradual cone a few feet over my head.

I grabbed two bars for balance, got to my feet and looked carefully down. The ground seemed far, far away. The field seemed to be moving in the darkness, surging like the ocean. Or . . . breathing.

I looked around me. I'd never seen Quiver from up this high, and it looked so different! Far to my left I could see the hazy golden lights of Foxgrape Woods, something you could never see from the ground. Far to my right rose the chat piles at the edge of Minetown, stark mountains of silver gravel taken from the zinc mines. Ahead of me was Route 66, wide and loud. Behind me were the houses on our block, their backs to the highway as though they were shocked by all that light and sound and movement.

I shut my eyes and took a deep breath of the wind.

"You're a woman now," I whispered. "You will never be a child again, not for one tiny second."

I expected bittersweet tears to overwhelm me, but instead, my eyes snapped open.

Where *were* all those cars going, and where *had* they all been?

I lifted my arms over my head, smiled in a flirty way, and began snapping my fingers and swaying. Dick Clark, handsome host of the hit TV show *American Bandstand*, appeared on the platform right beside me, raving into his microphone. *Hey, listen up all you hep cats and babydolls out there! Young Frannie Dee is about to top the charts and set the world of rock n' roll on fi-yur! Frannie, take it away, baby!*

"One o'clock, two o'clock, three o'clock ROCK!" I jumped, jerking my pelvis. "Four o'clock, five o'clock, six o'clock ROCK!" I jumped again as the crowd went wild.

Bright headlights swept across me as a car turned into the alley. It had to be Charlotte's boyfriend, Jay, coming to meet her! I dropped to my stomach on the platform, praying for dear life—*Please, please God, I'll do anything, just say no one saw me up here doing . . . what I was doing. Please! I won't write notes in church and I'll care about the fate of the free world! Anything! Pleeeese!*

But the car wasn't Jay. It was Mr. Chisholm and his daughter again! They stopped where they had the night before, flicked on those strong-beamed flashlights of theirs, and started working their way into the field. Pressing myself as flat as possible, I wriggled forward until I could see over the edge of the platform. *F.E. Driscoll here, ladies and gentlemen—on surveillance at a new and far riskier aerial location!*

Mr. Chisholm's daughter was kicking the weeds out sideways with each step, then crouching down to peer through them. Mr. Chisholm walked along slowly, bent far forward at the waist. "All right, here's the tree stump we located last night!" he suddenly called to her and Celeste ran over to him. I couldn't see any tree stump, but there was an uneven, dark circle of cinders I guess could have been one once. They stood together for a minute, talking too quietly for me to hear, then he lifted one arm and pointed and they walked in that direction for a few feet. When they reached their mysterious destination, they got down on their knees, balanced their flashlights beside them, and began yanking weeds and digging with their hands.

They worked for a long time. Mr. Chisholm picked up several tiny, rock-like things and pocketed them.

Then he found something bigger, something that must have been important because he sat back in the grass and held it close to his flashlight to look it over.

I got a quick, clear look at a little finger-sized piece of something ugly and black. Big deal—this field had been full of cinders ever since the car parts store burned down. On the other hand, what if that finger-shaped thing really was a . . . crusty, burned-up finger? I felt light-headed. *Breathe!* I ordered myself, and inched so far forward on the platform I nearly lost my balance and nose-dived right off.

Celeste had quit working to watch, and Mr. Chisholm carefully handed his discovery to her. She cradled it in both hands. He said in a low, grim voice, "I can hardly believe this is what I think it is, Celeste. We're definitely in the right place, though, so it very well could be." He took those little rock things out of his pocket and she leaned closer to look at them. He said, "This area would quite literally have been *soaked* in blood, and now seems blighted and cursed from the pure evil of . . . "

A wedding party took over the highway—happy, yelling and blaring horns. I nearly groaned in frustration. How did they expect me to hear?!

"People are experts at self-justification, Celeste," Mr. Chisholm was saying when the party noise finally faded into the distance. He took the awful black thing from

Celeste, then stood and held it carefully with his fingertips, looking down at it. "In the cold light of day people bury their sins quickly and turn their heads away. But the earth . . . the earth, as you see, is much slower to forgive and forget."

A few minutes later the Chisholms left, taking their grotesque discovery with them, and I scrambled down the ladder and ran home high-kneed and on tiptoe, suddenly remembering in gruesome detail stories people told about the Quiver Serpent, a Loch Ness-type monster that was trapped underground when the zinc mines were first dug. It now moved endlessly beneath Quiver and especially, some said, beneath this unlucky field, slithering around down there, wormlike and horrifying, arising suddenly out of nowhere to snap at your ankles. Or worse.

CHAPTER 6

The next morning, I got up earlier than I'd even planned to get up for the first day of school. I slid into the breakfast-table chair across from my dad. He was reading the morning paper and eating toast with peanut butter.

"Daddy, now, I want to ask you something, and I want you to tell me the straight truth, bearing in mind that I'm a woman and no longer a child, okay?" I kept my voice cool and sophisticated. "And, uh, don't worry, it's not about . . . Communists or anything."

He lowered his paper. "Peanut butter toast? I'll carve you up a banana onto a piece, just like you like it, Franniebananie."

"I guess," I said, rolling my eyes at that silly name he had for me.

He smiled. "Shoot. Ask away."

"Okay. Tell me the exact truth about when the zinc mines were first started." I concentrated on pouring myself some juice, though my blood was swishing noisily against my eardrums. "Was there really . . . something, a monster or something, trapped under them? I mean, that's obviously just some dumb old story. Right?"

He reached for a banana and started carving it paper-thin onto a piece of his peanut-buttered toast. "The mines were started a long time ago, Frannie—before the first World War, way back when there weren't very high-tech or safe ways of mining. I've heard guys at work talking about how parts of the tunnels would collapse down there every few days. Nothing major, at first. Then one day a whole section gave way, and some men were killed. Eleven, if I remember the story right. They couldn't reach their bodies, so they just left them buried there, deep inside the mine. I think those crazy old stories about a monster started with that cave-in. The guys at the plant who were telling this story said some of the Minetown people claimed to hear a slithering sound under where that part of the mine was sealed. It was just more of the gravel caving in, but I guess lots of people over near there were convinced it was some kind of giant snake sent to prowl the deep mine tunnels to avenge the deaths of those men."

"Avenge?" He pushed the toast over to me, and I started licking the bananas, a thing I loved to do if Mom wasn't at the table to stop me. "But why would they *need* avenging since it was just an accident? And why would people say the Quiver Serpent lurks under a field here in the middle of Quiver, instead of under Minetown, where the cave-in was?"

Daddy stood up and took his dishes to the sink. "Like I said, the snake's just a crazy story. I guess they had him slither over here to Quiver because the mine owners lived here. Only the miners themselves lived in Minetown."

"So the miners who were killed were probably Negroes and Indians, right? And the owners were probably white people, like now. Rich white people."

"Most likely," he answered. "A few white men probably worked the mines back then, just like now. But not many. You be sure and help your mother in the kitchen this week, Fran. She was up till all hours last night studying for that real estate test she's set her mind on taking."

"She wants to be a broker, not just Mr. Joslen's secretary," I murmured, carrying my own plate to the sink. "Daddy? What if that slithering sound was . . . was somebody still alive down there? I mean, did they really try *hard* to dig them out? Like they would have, I mean, if they'd been . . . white people?"

Daddy turned to me, smiling but shaking his head. "What questions! My two pretty women are thinking way too much lately." He draped the dishtowel over my shoulder. "Focus that brainpower on something useful, okay? Like putting away last night's dishes."

He winked good-bye and left, and I grabbed two handfuls of silverware from the drainer by the sink. As I dropped spoons and forks into the drawer, I could see the field out the kitchen window. It seemed like either a plain old weedy junkyard *or* a cursed and blood-soaked nether world, depending on how you looked at it.

Nobody likes to walk in alone the first day of school, so Kelly's dad brought her into town to my house that morning so we could walk the four blocks to Quiver Junior High together.

It was clear, white-skyed and already hot when we went outside. Kelly could walk forever without talking, but after a couple of blocks I couldn't keep my thoughts to myself any longer.

"Kelly? Can you think of any reason why there might be, uh . . . body parts in the field behind my house?" Trying to seem nonchalant, I waved to Mrs. Dolfer and her ugly little dog, who yapped angrily back at me. "Small body parts, I mean? Like, say . . . burned fingers?"

Anyone else would have driven me crazy asking why I'd asked that, but Kelly just frowned and started cracking her knuckles. After about half a block, she said, "No." Behind us, Mrs. Dolfer's terrier kept on yapping, throwing himself in vicious frustration against his chain-link fence.

I took a deep breath. "Well, uh, you know the girl I rescued from that dragonbee?"

Kelly looked at me. I could tell she was trying to decide whether to point out there hadn't been a dragonbee, but finally she just said, "The girl whose father you told us bought the spook house."

"Right. Well, there are some strange things about those two. I've been doing this . . . surveillance? But my results at this point are inconclusive."

"You mean you're going over to the old spook house and *spying* on them?"

"Of course not!" I'd been going to tell her about the field and what I'd overheard back there last night, but now that she'd used the word "spying" I was afraid she might misunderstand my surveillance as much as, say, my parents would have.

Max, Jason and Theodore went by in their go-cart. Max and Jason raised their arms and waved wildly to us, and Theodore gave us one majestic nod. Seeing Theodore reminded me of him scolding Nancy and me in church, which reminded me of my promise to God when I was in a pinch last night. But I just couldn't bring myself to care about the fate of the free world with all the first-day-of-school stuff I had to worry about right now.

We turned the corner from Jackson Street to Broken Bow Avenue, and suddenly there was our school, a big two-story rectangle of yellow brick surrounded by a few acres of trampled brown grass and a short stone wall that trapped everybody's discarded test papers and candy bar wrappers. I got that half-sick feeling that I knew from experience was a mixture of anticipation and nerves.

Kelly and I melted into the stream of kids heading through the big front doors. The halls and stairways at Quiver Junior High were wide and echoey, and the newly buffed dark blue floor tile had a promising look, deep and shiny as the ocean. All last year's graffiti had somehow been washed off the lockers, too, and they stood gleaming like fresh tablets, waiting for this year's layer of cleverness.

We got in line to get our schedules at the big enrollment table set up in front of the cafeteria. A new bright white sign had been hung on the wall there, where everybody would probably read it while waiting, bored, for their turn to eat. Inside a border of tiny American flags was printed: *"Ask not what your country can do for you; ask what you can do for your country."—President John Fitzgerald Kennedy.*

"President Kennedy said that when he got inaugurated last January," Kelly informed me, which, of course, everyone in the United States of America already knew.

I looked around, chewing my lip, waving to people who waved to me, trying not to be self-conscious. I would *not* bite my nails this year! I would *not*.

One of the big outside doors behind us squealed open and thudded shut, as it had every few seconds as new kids trailed in. But this time a silence began growing through the crowd of kids that stretched between the door and the enrollment table.

"What?" I asked Kelly, as that hush traveled up behind us like a tidal wave. I was afraid to turn around and see what had happened, but the big glass trophy case was a few yards in front of us, right behind the enrollment table. It made a perfect mirror, so I took a step sideways and looked into it.

A pretty girl was standing alone back by the doors. She was fairly tall and very slim, with a roll of bangs and her hair caught up sleekly at the sides in two barrettes. She was wearing penny loafers, white socks, a pleated skirt, and a soft, cloudlike white sweater. Her chin was high and she was smiling slightly, hugging her books to her chest but not trying to hide behind them like I did sometimes in new situations. Her nails were shiny with polish. That's how she looked all over— polished.

I know it must sound strange that I didn't recognize Celeste right away, but I'd only seen her through tinted car windows and in the shadowy field. You couldn't tell black from white in the trophy case mirror, so she looked just like Kelly and me, only prettier.

When I finally realized she was Celeste, it wasn't from how she looked, but from the way people behind her were shoving through the doors, then stopping as quickly as if they'd slammed into a brick wall and stepping wide around her.

While I stood staring at her in the trophy glass case, feeling hidden because I was looking in a mirror, she suddenly looked right back at *my* reflection, her eyes as wide and direct as they'd been through her father's car window. Flustered at being caught, I whirled toward her and awkwardly bobbed up one hand to wave.

Several people turned to stare at *me* then, so I jerked down my hand and stepped quickly back to my own place in line.

I ran into Theodore C. Rockman as we were both hurrying to find our new lockers, which turned out to be only a few feet apart.

"Did you see the new girl?" I asked him quickly. "Isn't she supposed to be at Carver? Margot says our school is restricted, like you told us Foxgrape Woods was."

"The proper term is 'segregated,'" Theodore informed me absentmindedly. He crouched down so his lock was at eye-level and began squinting at the combination he'd written on the palm of his hand. "And schools no longer are. Public schools have been integrated since Brown vs. the Board of Education back in 1954. Don't you remember reading that in our social studies book last year?"

He moved the dial on his lock gingerly to the left, to the right, and to the left again, but it wouldn't open. Various estimates put the good lock/bad lock ratio at our school somewhere between 50/50 and 40/60.

"I think we skipped that part in my class," I murmured. For the first time, it occurred to me that maybe we shouldn't have. I turned my full attention to my own lock, which opened easily, thank goodness. Inside, my new locker was gum-pocked and had the somehow comforting smell of moldy tennis shoes.

"I apparently must redesign you, you wretched thing," Theodore told his lock.

"But if our school has been, what's that word—integrated? If it's been that since we were all little kindergartners back in 1954, then why is Celeste our first Negro? Other kids at the edge of Minetown live as close to Quiver Junior High as to Carver."

Theodore looked up at me over the top of his glasses. "Apparently, they lack her bravery." He looked back down at his lock and took a tiny screw driver out of the plastic pen holder in his shirt pocket. "Or her foolishness. Just which remains to be seen."

CHAPTER 7

The rest of the day I didn't have one second to think about monster serpents or Robin or *anything.*

My seven classes were spread all over the building—I'd be a human pinball! Seven teachers, not a single one of whom I'd had back in seventh grade. Everybody said Coach Hinsdale let the football players get away with murder in his American history class, and the desk he assigned me was right in front of one of his tackles! My locker stuck a little at the bottom. How would I get into my gym uniform quickly enough after chorus, when the music room was clear across the building from the gym? Wouldn't my stomach growl in algebra, which would be a quiet class right before lunch?

"Maybe we should wait another week or so to do this," I suggested when Nancy, Margot, Kelly and I were working on the luau out on my patio late that afternoon.

"Why, mon cheri?" Margot asked.

"Everything's so hectic right now!" I answered. I stuck my hands back into the papier mâché mixture. It felt soothing to my chewed-to-the-quick fingernails.

"Everything's all set for us to have the luau Friday night," Nancy said in a flat don't-bother-arguing way. The rest of us were sitting on the humid concrete, but Nancy had brought along a folding deck chair for herself and an armload of her mother's recipe books, and she was sitting in the shade of the mimosa, sipping iced tea and marking recipes. Once in a while she looked over the tops of her rhinestone-studded sunglasses to be sure we were doing things right.

"Well, I've got too much on my mind already to have to take the blame if it's a big, fat flop," I informed her. "Just because it's on my patio doesn't mean you guys aren't totally responsible!"

I pulled over the volcanic rock I'd started the day before, and began layering it with more strips of papier mâché-coated newspaper. It was relaxing, in a way. I seemed to have a real talent for papier mâché sculpting. Whereas everyone else's rocks looked like beach balls, I'd been careful to give mine dents and crevasses, making them much more realistic. The palm tree trunks I'd made were realistic too, unlike most of the others, which resembled giant brown hot dogs.

Noted sculptor Fran Driscoll will open her newest exhibit

at a tea and brunch given by the Museum of Modern Art. R.S.V.P. or you will surely be excluded by an armed guard at the door from this magnificent, totally sophisticated artistic event.

"Fran-*nie!*"

"Huh? What?"

"I *said,* have you talked to Jason and Max and Theodore yet about not acting like themselves at the party?" Nancy asked. "And what about Celeste, that new girl?"

A little sizzle went through me—I *had* thought about Celeste several times since my awkward wave at the beginning of the day. She was in three of my classes, all electives, and I'd thought about how that meant she was interested in the same things I was. Chorus, typing, and yearbook staff.

"What about her?" Kelly drawled. She'd just finished the palm tree she'd been working on and was now weaving mimosa blossoms into Nibbles' mane, experimenting. Nancy had told her Nibbles could come to the party, but only if she was decorated.

"Nobody *talks* to her," Margot said, "Everybody *avoids* her like there's an invisible forcefield around her. So . . . do we invite her?"

Margot had that exactly right. It *was* like Celeste was inside a forcefield, a clear plastic bubble that kept people several feet away. It was almost *visible* when she walked down the halls. In chorus she sat in the last chair on the second row, and the girl nearest her had automatically swiveled her chair so her back was turned slightly toward her.

"Don't look at *me*, Nancy," I said, because that's exactly what Nancy was doing—looking at *me* over the tops of those sunglasses of hers. "*I'm* not doing it."

It was ridiculous how people were acting, and *someone* needed to be nice to Celeste, but that someone was *not* me. That one tiny wave this morning had made everybody stare, which was the last thing I needed. Besides, Celeste probably thought there hadn't even been a dragonbee, so she probably assumed I was a big liar. And for all I knew, she might have seen me spying on her and her dad from my window or the rocket. Doing surveillance, I mean. If I was going to live through the year with this killer schedule, I couldn't chance having somebody call me a liar or a spy right in front of everybody.

Kelly said, "We'll just put an invitation in Celeste's locker, like we do in everybody else's."

Suddenly, things got too quiet. Not just nothing-to-say quiet. Tense quiet.

"You guys don't want to invite her," Kelly stated.

Margot put her hands on her hips. "I didn't say that! Did I say that? I DID NOT SAY THAT!" She threw up her arms dramatically. "I would absolutely ADORE to invite her, but this party is *only* about the most important and the trickiest thing we've ever tried to do. We'll have to be the ones that make her feel at home, and it's hard to even know what to talk to her about. You never see a colored girl on a Maybelline or Revlon commercial. Do they use hair spray? Do they wear hose? Do they eat Wheaties? You never see one on a pet food commercial. Do they have pets?"

"Of *course* they have pets, Margot," Nancy said, swirling the ice in her drink.

"I still say you're mostly worried about someone at the party calling her a bad name or something," Kelly muttered.

"Kelly, you should go to church," Nancy scolded. "It isn't Christian to *think* like that."

"It's not like *Kelly's* the one who's thinking about calling her a bad name, Nancy," I translated quietly. "Kelly's just saying *somebody* might."

"Wise up, Nancy," Kelly advised. "Several people who came out to do ranch business with my dad today asked him if that *nigger* girl was really going to my school."

I flinched. People, mostly adults, used that word all the time around here, usually making jokes. The gas station guys, the ladies at the beauty shop, the waitresses at Skif's. Quiver was a nice town where people joked around with their neighbors, and using that word was a way of doing that. It was sort of tasteless, and our mothers told us not to do it, but on the other hand they told us not to be rude and correct our elders who were doing it.

"Just smile politely but don't listen," Nancy said, stubbornly raising her chin and fanning her neck with her hand.

"I *don't* listen." This was the very first time I'd seen Kelly angry, except of course when someone criticized her horse. "What difference does that make? People not listening doesn't stop ignorant people! Smart people mostly keep their minds on their business, but ignorant people like to hang around the corral and talk, and they just talk louder and longer when they can tell you wish they'd shut up! Boy, it's obvious you guys haven't spent much time around ranchers."

"Don't lump *me* with those ignorant bigots," Margot said hotly. "All *I* meant was, we won't know how to talk to Celeste!"

"Well, my mother says those silly riots they're having down there in the far south are because people don't remember that sticks and stones may break your bones but words will never hurt you," Nancy told us in this preachy voice, turning the pages of her recipe book in a fast, no-nonsense way. "If people would remember that, everyone could just get along and the world would be a better place."

"So, Nancy, you're saying it's okay to call someone a

name they hate just to make yourself feel like a big shot?" Kelly asked. Her cheekbones looked sharp and dangerous.

"No," Nancy said and slammed the book shut. "I'm *merely* saying it's nothing personal! If somebody *does* use a word like that, a colored person should just ignore it in her heart."

"Negroes have to sit in the back of busses in some places," I pointed out. That was a fact I'd accidentally picked up while the TV news was pointed toward us at dinner a few nights ago.

"Maybe it's nice in the back," Margot suggested, shrugging. "Why wouldn't it be?"

"And some places have separate restrooms for colored people and white people, and separate drinking fountains," I added. I smoothed the same piece of soggy, dissolving newspaper for about the twentieth time. "Separate everything."

"But not *here* we don't," Nancy pronounced. "Quiver is a nice town, where people are Christians and that's that!"

One of my thumbs suddenly went through my rock, clear to the chicken wire foundation. I stuck the other thumb in to widen the damage.

"You don't know everything that's ever happened here, Nancy," I heard myself mumble. Blood was swishing against my eardrums, and I tried my best not to glance between the slots in the patio fence, where I might just see the Quiver Serpent looking for prey, avenging those miners.

"And what's *that* supposed to mean?" Nancy shot back.

Without a word, Kelly stood up and stormed off the patio. In the yard, she turned on her boot heel and came back. "By the way, Margot, I've been meaning to tell you. That piece of shade you hog over there by the fence? It's mine. You get up and go sit there in the sun where the papier mâché glop is sticking to the concrete. Who knows? Maybe it's *nice* over there in the smelly, sticky one hundred-degree heat."

She turned again then, and was gone for good. I couldn't tell for sure whether Margot got her point. All she said was, "Le crazy! Crazy femme a la horse! Cra-zy!"

My rock was now a useless, sticky, wiry pulp. Why did Nancy get to lord over everybody from that nice, cool chair? Oh, sure, she said she had a delicate system and was prone to sunstroke, but did that give her the right to act like the only living Christian in the entire world? And why couldn't Kelly say things in a more cautious, less blunt and cowgirly way? Why couldn't Margot stick to English? Why was it so windy and hot, hot, hot?

In the heat, the pink blooms of the mimosa trees, which, if I remembered correctly, had been about the main reason we were having this stupid luau in the first place, were sizzling away to sticky globs that looked exactly like chewed bubblegum.

I usually lost interest and went on to bed when Jay and Charlotte disappeared into his Chevy each night, but that night I kept watching from my window even after Charlotte re-emerged from the back seat twenty minutes later and skulked back through her yard, her beehive hairdo a complicated, lopsided mess.

I watched the alley till nearly midnight, but Celeste and her father didn't show up.

Then, sleepy but still restless, I shifted my gaze to the headlights on Route 66. For all the nine years we'd lived in Quiver, I'd watched that endless parade of cars and wondered why those people didn't snap out of it and realize they should stop and stay right here in Quiver, where, like Nancy had said, it was so nice.

But why did we have to smile along at ignorant, unfunny jokes forever and ever? And if people really believed words didn't hurt you, why'd they teach their little kids that sticks-and-stones rhyme? If something didn't hurt you, you didn't have to tell yourself in a rhyme that it didn't. It just . . . *didn't.*

I tumbled to my side, hugging my pillow, frightened by my own disloyalty. Thinking for a single minute that your town wasn't perfect was pretty darn unpatriotic. Not as bad as calling Americans Communists, but still, pretty darn bad.

Oh Robin, Robin, life is so complicated! Where are you tonight when I need you so desperately?

Ah, my Francina, I long to hold you in my muscular arms, but alas, Bruce Wayne and I are out in the Batmobile crime fighting in faraway Berlin, securing the future of democracy and the entire free world . . .

CHAPTER 8

I was rushing to my third-hour choir class the next morning when I saw Max, Jason and Theodore standing together in front of the trophy case like they were just waiting to be humiliated by someone they thought of as a friend.

"Hi, guys. Uh, listen, I've been meaning to talk to you about—"

"Frannie!" Max interrupted excitedly. "Look! The trophy Theodore and Jason won last spring just got back from the engravers!"

Sure enough, there it was, a small wooden shield with a brass plaque on the front reading "FIRST PLACE IN TEAM DEBATE, STATE SPEECH CONTEST Spring, 1961." It was propped in the back right corner of the bottom shelf as though cowering in fright beneath the dense forest of huge football, track, and basketball trophies.

"Congratulations!" I said. "Max, weren't they supposed to put that gold medal you won in extemporaneous speaking in there, too?"

Max sighed. "Actually, I accidentally used it in a soda machine on the way home from the contest, thinking it was a quarter."

I nodded sympathetically, then plunged in. "Uh, listen, I wanted to tell you guys something real quick. I . . . I mean, two things. First, you're invited to a party, on my patio this Friday. A luau. And the second thing is, well, we're . . . we're requesting that no one drive private vehicles. Such as cars or go-carts. Because of, well, limited parking space."

Theodore raised his eyebrows and looked at me suspiciously over the top of his glasses. I had to finish this, fast!

"And we're also requesting that no one bring, well, rectangular things, such as, oh, say, chess boards. Or . . . news magazines. Or . . . or briefcases. Again, there's just such limited space, since we'll be having all these refreshments and palm trees and stuff, and a . . . a possible decorated horse."

Stupid! Stupid! Stupid! I was going to *brain* Nancy the very next time I saw her.

By then, I couldn't meet anyone's eyes. "The trophy looks great!" I chirped and hurried, head down, on to chorus.

As it turned out, I was rushing headlong into what Walter Cronkite might have called a fast-breaking disaster.

"Young ladies and gentlemen," Miss Cantwell announced as soon as the bell rang and the choir room door was closed so tightly that all chance of last-minute escape was past, "today I'm going to have you each sing a short melody by yourselves in front of the rest of the class so I can get a better idea of your individual vocal range."

Everyone began blathering out panicky excuses ranging from strep throat to needing to immediately change their schedules to take shop class.

"I anticipated resistance to this," Miss Cantwell said, smiling as sweetly as a nurse who's just snuck up on you with a giant shot needle, "so we'll get it over with quickly. We'll start with the sopranos. I want you each in turn to stand, face the class, and sing the first four lines of the familiar song on page seventeen of your chorus books."

The song on page seventeen was the title song from the Broadway musical *Oklahoma!,* which might not be a familiar song anywhere else in the world, but definitely is in Oklahoma. I was seven people down on the first row of sopranos, which meant that by the time she got to me, I'd had time to imagine several horrible possibilities. Would I freeze up and forget how to read English? Had anyone ever vomited while singing?

I stood on spaghetti legs, but when I'd finished the

four lines I hadn't done anything totally humiliating and I was even pretty sure I hadn't sounded half as awful as at least three or four of the people before me had. I sank down to my chair, dizzy with relief.

Celeste was the last soprano to sing because, like I said, she sat at the very end of the second row. Before she started, she took a little step away from her chair. The rest of us had tried for a sort of half-seated slouch with the backs of our legs *against* our chairs so it wasn't so obvious we were the only one standing. She also held her music book down and out from her body.

While Miss Cantwell played the opening chords, Celeste squared her shoulders and raised her chin. She seemed to get taller. She reminded me of something—I later figured out it was a picture we had in a book at home of a majestic Egyptian queen reading a scroll to her subjects. Though some of the girls tore their eyes away long enough to roll them at each other, I noticed they looked immediately back at her afterwards. She was an eye magnet.

And then, she sang. When she finished, no one seemed to be breathing.

Miss Cantwell had turned to stone, her eyes glassy and her mouth open.

"Thank you," she finally whispered, in a voice like someone would use to thank a person who had just donated a lifesaving kidney to them.

It was as though she was thanking Celeste not just for being so wonderful, but for restoring her faith in music and even humanity itself, at least the junior high variety.

Like most of the other girls, I hurried to the rest room after choir. That day I happened to notice Celeste going into one of the stalls right before I went into mine. Some other girls came in then, and talked in front of the big double mirrors.

"She's unbelievable," Patsy Dunn said. "Where'd she come from, Tulsa or someplace?"

"*Some* city I bet," Tricia Harmon answered. "She must have had *les*sons."

"Yeah, *les*sons," the others agreed, like that was unfair.

"She'd be pretty good, but that attitude of hers just ruins it," Tricia went on. "Like the way she just stands so *out* there, like she owns the whole world or something. My mother says she wouldn't *be* at our school if she didn't have a chip on her shoulder to start with. Just because it's legal now to mix schools doesn't make it right or natural, is what my father says."

"Mine too, almost those same words," Patsy said.

"Just her and her dad are here in Quiver," Carla Foster added. "I heard her mother's in jail someplace. Tulsa, I guess. Her dad's here to stir things up, is what *my* dad said."

"Stir what?" Tammy asked.

"Oh, you know," Tricia answered. "Just stir up bad things, like they've got in Tulsa."

They fluttered back out the door, still talking. I didn't dare leave my stall until after I saw Celeste's feet leaving hers, stopping at the sink, then going on out the door.

As I quickly ran my own hands under the sputtery water faucet, I imagined I'd just overheard them saying about me what they'd been saying about Celeste. I felt my face clench, like I'd been kneed in the stomach.

I shoved out the door and pretty much ran down the hall. I spotted Celeste ahead of me, walking fast, maneuvering around people with her head down.

I followed her up the stairs, staying a careful few yards behind her, and when she started to turn into her classroom, I shocked myself completely by calling, "Celeste? Wait up a second."

She stopped and looked back over her shoulder. Her face was smooth and beautiful and calm. I couldn't read any expression, though she'd surely heard everything I had.

I ran up closer, my heart pounding.

"Hi. I just wanted to tell you real quick—some friends and I are having a party Friday night, at my house. You'll get an invitation in your locker Thursday, but I just wanted to tell you personally, just so, well, you'd know who was having it. Me, I mean. I'm having it, with some friends. I'm . . . Frannie Driscoll."

"You're the one who pretended to kill that bug on my car," she said.

Pretended! So she *did* think I was a liar! "I . . . I better get to class," I stammered, then turned and fled.

I didn't go to class, though. I felt shaky and weak and my mind was racing, so I faked having cramps to get out of PE and sat in the library. I meant to study my American history, but I ended up just chewing my fingernails until it was time to go to algebra.

CHAPTER 9

I was glad everybody was still too mad from yesterday's big argument to work on the luau that afternoon, because I really wanted to skate in private. I had some thinking to do that seemed too urgent to wait for my usual spying-on-Charlotte thinking time.

Since there wasn't an inch of room left on the patio, I had to skate and think in the basement, which had two big drawbacks. One, the floor down there was too rough for the wooden wheels of my new shoeskates, and two, my dead salamander had been down there since July in a Folger's coffee can.

I crept to the bottom basement step and sat using my old skate key to tighten my old metal-wheeled clamp-on skates to my loafers. "Janice, are you listening?" I whispered. "Do you forgive me for not feeding you?"

The basement was empty except for Mom's washer

and dryer, and the Folger's can over in the dim shadows of the corner.

"I meant to, Janice. I just kept forgetting." That was a lie and I knew it. I stood and skated once around the room, trying not to look at the coffee can, getting used to the uneven floor and the wobbly feel of my old skates.

"You are a horrible, horrible person, Frannie Driscoll," I said out loud, skating faster. "You're a pet murderer and a spy and there's no such *thing* as a dragonbee!"

There was a big pipe running from floor to ceiling through the middle of the basement. I grabbed it, pointed my toes outward, pumped to go around, and began singing dramatically from the very depths of my misery and pain. I pictured myself looking and sounding like Celeste.

"O-O-O-O-O-O-O-Oklahoma where the wind comes sweeping down the plain! And the wa-ving WHEAT! Can sure smell SWEET! When the wind comes right behind the RA-A-A–A-A-IN! Oh, Oh, Oh, O-O-O-O-Oklahoma every night my honeylamb and I! Sit alone and TALK! or watch a HAWK! makin' LA-ZEE-CIRcles in the SKY!"

In an intensely moving performance, even though her heart is clearly breaking, Francine Driscoll has yet again proven why she's beloved throughout the world of skating as well as the world of music, sports fans! Never a misstep, never a moment when she appears out of control or awkward. Un-be-lievable poise. Just unbelievable!

I was taking off my skates an hour or so later when my mother came down the stairs with a load of laundry.

"Mom, are there bad things in Tulsa?" I asked.

"Tulsa?" she said, swinging the laundry basket up to the lid of the washer. "My cousin Twila just *adores* the new shopping center there. It's got a roof right over the whole entire thing, if you can even picture that."

"I don't mean shopping. Are there bad thoughts or attitudes or something like that in Tulsa that someone might want to start up here for some reason? I mean, like, if they had a chip on their shoulder or something?"

She waited till the clothes had all tumbled into the washer to answer.

"Well, Frannie, I do believe people in cities tend to think a little bit too much," she said slowly. "By which I mean that sometimes it's better to just leave things well enough alone instead of always . . . agitating."

I chewed my lip. "Who decides what's well enough, though? I mean, just because things are well enough for some people doesn't mean they are for everybody. Does it?"

"Frannie, you've lost me," she said as she measured detergent. "I'm sure I don't know *what* you're talking about."

"I'm talking about who gets to decide what's right and natural. Does the majority get to decide? I mean, is it like you take a vote or something? Or does God do it and everybody just plays along and keeps quiet?"

She banged the lid closed and adjusted the knob that started the water. "There's something a little more immediate I think we should be talking about, Fran. This party you're having here Friday. It doesn't seem all that well organized to me. You're inviting the whole eighth grade class?"

I shrugged. "That's what everybody does when they have a party."

"And they'll be *eating* here?"

I shrugged. "Everybody has food at their parties. But don't worry, Mom, Nancy's got the menu all figured out."

"I wish I knew who this everybody was you're always talking about," she murmured, shaking her head. Then she put the detergent into the empty basket, balanced it on her hip again, and hustled past me in a busy way. "Honey, take that old coffee can upstairs with you and throw it in the trash, would you please? I don't know what it's been doing down here all summer. If I'm going to pass my real estate license test next month I can't do every little thing around here all by myself."

I gulped. "Okay."

I tied my skate straps together and slung them over my shoulder, then picked the can up with both hands, carrying it far out in front of me.

I took it outside and put it down on the hot concrete of the patio where the bright white light gave me nerve enough to look inside. The last time I'd seen Janice was back in July, when I'd finally brought down a carrot for her and found her looking like a piece of curved, gray foam rubber, obviously deceased.

She was still curved like that, of course, but tiny now and darker looking, like a dried-up burned finger.

The next morning, my brother Mitch hit me in the eye with his sock while I was helping him put on his shoes. In chorus class I was still dabbing at that watery eye and only halfway listening when Miss Cantwell read off a list of people, and I heard my name.

"What?" I whispered urgently to this girl named Teresa who sat next to me.

"You're on the list of good singers," Teresa whispered back.

"I'd like all the people whose names I just read to meet with me briefly in the music room right after lunch today," Miss Cantwell concluded. "We'll start planning some small ensemble work!"

For the next two hours I felt like I was going to explode. "You guys, you guys!" I called out as I skidded up to my friends outside the cafeteria at lunch break. "I'm on Miss Cantwell's good singers list! I'm on Miss Cantwell's good singers list!"

Kelly gave me a congratulatory punch on the arm

and they all three acted happy for me, though Margot said, "Christina Jenson told me just about everybody was on it."

Christina Jenson had exaggerated. Only about *half* the chorus class was on the good singers list—seven of us sopranos out of a possible thirteen. When we went back to the music room after lunch, Miss Cantwell explained to us that she wanted to form the good singers into a few "training ensembles" and one "performance ensemble." The performance ensemble would be the best of the best—a girls' double trio, which would probably perform in public this very semester.

Tricia Harmon raised her hand. "Miss Cantwell? Have you chosen the six girls?"

"We'll have auditions some day next week," Miss Cantwell said.

It was easy to figure out who would be in it. Tricia and Celeste would be the two sopranos. Jackie and Tanya, or maybe Brenda, would be the two altos. The two second sopranos would be Tanya or Brenda, whichever one wasn't an alto, and Carla or Diane or Denise.

And I'd be in a training ensemble. A training ensemble! I decided to try and briefly forget about it so that I could suddenly remember the wonderfulness of it all over again.

The bell rang and everyone grabbed their stuff and shoved quickly toward the door.

"Frannie?"

I whirled around. Celeste was standing alone near the piano, hugging her books and jiggling her left knee. Everyone elbowed on past me, and Miss Cantwell bustled into the little office cubicle she shared with the band teacher. Suddenly, Celeste and I were the only two people left in the room.

"Hi," I said nervously, walking closer. My heart raced—was this when she'd accuse me of lying, or even spying?

"I wanted to tell you, Frannie." She lifted her chin a little. "I wanted to tell you that my mama isn't in jail. She's a nurse, in St. Louis. Where we live. Lived."

"Oh," I said, gulping. "That's good."

"You probably heard those girls talking in the restroom yesterday, but they were wrong. Mama's a nurse at St. Luke's, and Dad's a teacher. He's on sabbatical."

"Oh," I repeated. I had no idea what a sabbatical was. "That's good," I said, hoping I was right.

Celeste looked down and picked at the sleeve of her sweater. "It was nice of you to invite me to your party. Don't worry, I won't be coming, but it was still nice."

It suddenly got sort of dark—the overhead lights were off, and a cloud must have covered the sun.

Celeste flicked her eyes up to meet mine, as if waiting for me to say something. I saw they had little flecks of shiny gold in the irises.

"Frannie, why would they make up something like that about my mother?" she asked softly.

Her question caught me totally by surprise.

"Oh, you know, they were just, like, talking," I babbled, groping, saying anything. "I mean, those girls accuse my friend Kelly of peroxiding her hair every week, but it's just white like that because she spends all her time on a horse in the sun."

I hadn't come all that close to answering her question, but Celeste nodded and smiled. "Anyway, I wanted to say thanks about the invitation," she repeated.

"Okay!" I jerked my shoulders up in a cheerful shrug. "Well, gotta run!"

And I did, literally, run all the way to my locker, where I crammed my morning books in, snatched my afternoon books out, slammed the door and ran on to my next class.

I was the first one there, of course—all that running. I put my head down on my desk and scrinched shut my eyes, wondering if I was going to survive the constant emotional roller coaster of one single week of eighth grade.

CHAPTER 10

We worked on my patio for a while that afternoon. Everybody was pretty quiet, ground down by the first-week pressures of school. I guess Margot felt guilty about sounding like the whole world was on the good singers list, because she finally asked, "How'd your special meeting with Miss Cantwell go, mon cheri?"

I shrugged, concentrating on the lei I was winding. "It went okay. I've been meaning to tell you guys, I talked to Celeste about the party. She said it was nice of us to invite her, but she's probably not coming."

I felt Kelly looking at me.

"You know," I mumbled, squinting down at my tangled mess of a lei, "what I don't get is, why do we spend all our classtime learning all this relatively useless stuff like algebra? It seems like we should be learning how to, you know . . . how to just *be.*"

"What were her exact words?" Kelly asked.

I threw down the lei. "How should *I* know? You expect me to remember every single word of every single conversation I've had in my lifetime?" I pulled up my knees, put my arms around them, and said more quietly, "I think she said, 'Don't worry, I probably won't be coming.' "

"Don't . . . worry?" Margot repeated.

I nodded, then put my forehead on my knees so I wouldn't have to look at anybody.

"You *were* worried, Margot," Kelly said. "Remember?"

No one said anything for a while. Kelly quit working and got up on Nibbles, then drooped forward and rested her head against Nibbles' neck. I picked up my lei and tried to rework it, but I couldn't concentrate at all. "I forgot, Nancy," I finally mumbled, tossing the lei aside again. "I also warned Jason, Max and Theodore not to act smart, just like you kept ordering me to."

"I don't give orders," Nancy said. "But thank you. Now, Frannie, since you're not working at anything, please hand me that empty coffee can that's over there by the fence."

I wanted to tell her that I wasn't her royal servant, that she could just stagger up to her own two lazy, ladylike feet. But I controlled myself and just asked, "What for?"

"I'm going to mix up more papier mâché. The moon needs more layers."

I glared at the dinky lopsided moon, dangling six feet above the water spigot. Why wasn't I telling her that the Folger's can wasn't exactly empty?

Instead, I heard myself offer in a too-sweet voice, "I'll mix it for you."

Horrified at my own actions, I took the Folgers can over to the spigot, poured a couple inches of dry plaster into it, then dribbled water over that. It was all I could do to stir the stuff around with a mimosa stick, but bossy Nancy would be reaching into it time and time again with her soft, pink fingers, pulling strip after strip of yellow crepe paper right across Janice's submerged and possibly even *dissolving* carcass.

Nancy told us we each had to make twenty-three invitations that night. We were supposed to use brown construction paper to make little folders with the invitation inside—"Aloha! Come to a luau! 312 Center Avenue, 8:00 Friday night!" Then we were supposed to make green construction paper palm trees to decorate the fronts.

Twenty-three invitations take a long time to make. By the last ten or so it was late and I was working in bed. My palm trees had become mere blobs that looked like green nuclear mushroom clouds. I didn't care. I just wanted to be *finished.*

There was a rough, romantic wind that night, the kind of wind that filled you with mysterious longings as you watched the dark clouds sail across the moon while the mimosa trees tossed themselves like dancers and Jay and Charlotte stood out there in the alley, passionately lip-locked. I began a mental letter to Robin as I glued those last two nuclear palms.

My darling, though I know the fate of the entire free world is on the shoulders of your strong, muscular arms, still I miss you so much and East Berlin seems half a world away! I have thrilling news—I've been chosen to perform in a quite select training ensemble. Yet I am so often confused, my love. You see, once I starved a beloved pet. And when I talk to people I seem to sound quite stupid sometimes. Another enigma—I invited an intriguing stranger to a supposed luau, then was relieved when she announced she wouldn't be coming.

I froze with the glue bottle halfway squeezed.

I *had* been relieved.

For one tiny second before I forgot it, I had a little brain blip of insight about how we all used Nancy. She looked and thought and acted so much like a mother that we felt free to leave the hard decisions to her, then we could roll our eyes and blame her if something went wrong, like we did with our own mothers.

But *I'd* been the one in that music room alone with Celeste today, and she *was* intriguing and nice, and if I hadn't still been worried about how her being at the party would make things hard I could have tried to persuade her to change her mind and come.

"Charlotte, you get your sorry self into this house or you'll wisht you had!"

Thankful to have my thoughts interrupted, even by Charlotte's yelling father, I flopped over onto my stomach, pulled my pillow over my head and tried to get to sleep.

At about dawn, I wandered in my pajamas out onto the patio. I owed Janice a decent burial in a shoebox, not just being thrown into the dumpster in that gloppy Folger's can.

I turned the can over and pounded the bottom until the three-inch piece of solid plaster that held Janice fell out. It was easier than I thought it would be to free her. I just hit the plaster with a rock and she tumbled out like a pit from the center of a peach. I looked at her lying there, then decided I just wasn't in the mood to bury her, so I put her back in the empty can and shoved the can under the card table we'd put up on the patio.

I forced myself to look out at the field, then. No monster snake was curled around the bars of the rocket or anything. But it probably wouldn't be, in the daylight.

CHAPTER 11

I felt grouchy and disoriented all that morning. When I saw Celeste in choir, I snuck her an unobtrusive wave, then worried that she'd *know* I'd meant for it to be unobtrusive.

"Next Tuesday we'll have after-school tryouts for anyone interested in being in the girls' select double trio," Miss Cantwell announced.

Four boys immediately bounced in their chairs and shot up their hands, but Miss Cantwell pretended not to see them. "I shouldn't have said 'anyone.' Only girls, of course," she corrected, spoiling their hilarious joke.

In addition to my brain feeling filled with sludge, my bangs were trying to curve the wrong way that day, so after choir I went to the rest room to fix them. By that fourth day of school, Tricia Harmon and her friends had the middle of the mirror permanently staked out, so I went to the last sink.

"Carla's voice will blend best with ours," Tricia was saying to Tanya. "Denise is good, but she doesn't sing out. No offense, Denise."

Denise was holding a section of her hair above her head and running her comb up and down to tangle it. "Why should I care? I don't want to be in it," she said.

"So that's . . . okay . . . you and me for first soprano, Carla for second, and Jackie and Brenda for alto," Tanya said to Tricia. "Anybody got gum?"

"I do," Denise said. Leaving her comb stuck inside that hair tangle, she rummaged through her purse and found a tattered piece of grape bubblegum, which she threw across to Tricia. "Okay, you guys, at the beauty shop where my mother works, the Cultured Curl? This, what I'm doing here? Well, they do it all the time now. It's called ratting. It gives you gobs of hair. Okay, is everybody watching?"

She didn't mean me by "everybody," but I watched anyway from the corners of my eyes as she smoothed over the top of the tangle into a bump of hair on top of her head.

"Wow." Tanya nodded, smacking her gum. "Ratting, huh? That's better than a French twist."

"Nah, a twist is more elegant and stuff," Carla said. "And who's singing second soprano with me? Because not that Celeste girl. I'm not singing next to a convict."

I checked in the mirror. Celeste's feet were showing under one of the stall doors. Why couldn't Carla see that and *just shut up?*

And then something shocking occurred to me. Maybe they *did* see Celeste's feet.

"Her *mother's* the convict," Tanya corrected, and everyone giggled.

"Big dif!" Tricia said, causing more laughter. She leaned across to me. "Frannie, you should try out for second."

"Please?" Carla turned to me, her hands clasped together, pleading. "Save me from the convict! Pretty, pretty please?"

I cleared my throat. My voice still sounded croaky and my head was pounding.

"Well, but Miss Cantwell is picking, and no matter how many other people try out she'll surely pick Celeste, since she's so, you know. Good. And . . . don't worry, Carla, her mother's not a convict. She's a nurse, in St. Louis."

My heart was thudding and I could feel my neck getting blotchy red. I pretended to be concentrating on my bangs, but I could see Denise rolling her eyes and Carla smiling her who-does-she-think-she-is smile about me.

"Miss Cantwell works for the taxpayers, remember, Frannie?" Tricia told me in an ice-cold voice, leaning toward the mirror and smoothing her eyebrows up with her little fingers. "So it's not like her opinion's the law or anything. What's natural is natural, and what's not is not. You've got to think about the blend, and Celeste doesn't blend at all."

"*Way* doesn't blend," Tanya added.

"At *all*," Carla said.

They picked up their stuff then and left without glancing in my direction. In the hall they'd talk about me. Any second now I'd be engulfed by the kind of sickening humiliation you felt when you made a fool of yourself around boys or popular people.

Celeste came out and started quietly washing her hands. I concentrated on fixing my bangs. She glanced up. Our eyes met in the mirror, and the short, uncontrolled smile she flashed me cut through my haze of misery and snapped me to attention like a slap. For that couple of seconds, with her eyes crinkled and one top tooth pushing out at her lip, she seemed like a totally different person. Less like a perfect Egyptian princess, and more like . . . something. What?

"Thanks," she said. "For setting them straight about my mother."

I shrugged, then swallowed. "By the way, I couldn't help noticing that the other day, uh, you said I 'pretended' to kill that dragonbee, you know? And I was recently thinking about that, and I thought I should explain that my eyesight is occasionally distorted by bright sunlight, so I did, at first, fully believe there was a deadly dragonbee on your window. So, in other words, I wasn't, uh, pretending. Or . . . or lying."

She looked at me and smiled that smile again. "I never thought it was lying. I just thought it was pretty creative." She pulled out a paper towel and started drying her hands. "Is there even such a thing as a dragonbee?"

Of course, I started to say. "No," I heard myself admit. I snorted a laugh, which should have been embarrassing. But it had been so long since I'd laughed at myself that it took me a second to figure out what was happening, and by then, she was laughing, too.

"Why'd you make it up, then?" she asked, still laughing a little.

"Who knows? I guess I was afraid you'd think I was some kind of homicidal maniac. I'm always worrying about what people think."

I couldn't believe I'd just told her that! That was twice in thirty seconds I'd told her embarrassing stuff about myself that even *I* barely knew.

"Frannie, tell me the truth," she said, then picked up her books from the sink and brushed some water drips from them. "Is everyone acting like they're acting because of my personality or something, or just because I'm the first colored girl to go to this school?"

"I haven't noticed anybody acting any way, except

stuck-up Tricia and her friends. Everybody normal thinks you're really neat!"

She wrapped her arms around her books and squeezed them to her chest. "I *know* everyone's avoiding me, Frannie."

I concentrated on pulling hairs from my brush as long as I could, then I cleared my throat. "I think it's just that . . . you're the first colored girl. I don't think people here are all that used to things being different than they're used to."

She nodded, understanding me even though I hadn't made much sense.

"At my old school in St. Louis there were colored kids and white kids," she said. "Way more white. Things came up that would hurt someone's feelings or make someone mad. But this being ignored like you'll just go away is new."

"Tricia and those girls are mostly just jealous because you sing like an angel."

"Thanks." She looked down and shook her head. "They're the reason I'm not trying out for double trio."

"But you *have* to!" I blurted.

She shook her head more firmly. "*You* try out," she said. "You're good enough to make it. Give them a run for their money."

I was stunned, but then I realized she must have been just joking.

"Not in a million years," I said with a whoop. "No way, Jose."

Celeste smiled at me again, then walked to the door. "It's almost time for the bell," she said.

I took a deep breath. "Celeste? I know you said you probably wouldn't be coming to our luau tomorrow night, but I wanted to be sure you know that all of us really want you to. If you can, that is."

She looked solemnly back at me for a few long seconds, then shrugged. "Maybe."

She kept standing there, her hand on the door, as though waiting for something.

My heart was racing so fast it was hard to concentrate. I frowned at my forehead in the mirror. "I guess I better give these hopeless bangs one more try."

"Okay, see you," she said, then raised her chin and slipped that smooth, calm princess face of hers on again like a beautiful mask.

When she was gone, I scrinched my eyes shut and covered my face with my hands.

"I'm positive some of Kelly's invitations had horse slobber on them," Nancy confided to me for the fourth or fifth time as we slid the invitations into the lockers after lunch.

"Oh, Nancy, that's just pathetic and stupid!" I snapped. She and I were doing both sides of one hall, and

Kelly and Margot were doing the hall around the corner. "Kelly probably just put a cold bottle of pop down on the table where she was working last night and the condensation got her paper wet. And anyway, who *cares?*"

Nancy considered what I'd said, then yelled, "Kelly, some of your invitations are wrinkly! Like they were in something . . . wet!"

"I know," Kelly yelled back from around the corner. "It's horse slobber."

I bounced my forehead against the locker I was doing.

"Slow-*bare?!*" Margot screeched from around the corner. "Le slowbare de la *horse?*"

"Just shut up, Margot!" I heard myself yelling. "If you can't talk real French, just DON'T TALK IT AT ALL!"

What was *wrong* with me?

I punched the locker door with both fists, then stuck my burning knuckles quickly under my armpits, whirled around, and slid down to sit on the floor with my back pressed against the cold metal door. Even with my eyes squeezed shut, I could feel Kelly and Margot hurrying over, and I knew Nancy was towering above me like the Statue of Liberty.

"Don't even look at me!" I shrieked. "I'm just sick to death of people looking at me and looking at me all the time!"

★   ★   ★

In spite of my horrible mood, the three of them trailed home behind me that afternoon. After all, we *had* to get the patio finished. But it began to rain shortly after we started, and we had our hands full dragging all the decorations into my crammed garage. Then Margot called her brother and he picked everybody up and took them home.

The rain kept up. That night the field was a spooky, misty haze, and the cars along the highway seemed to be disintegrating.

Jay and Charlotte had the Chevy's windows so completely steamed up you could have taken your finger and practiced multiplication tables on them.

The wind changed direction, and I bounced onto my knees to close my window, then stayed kneeling there, studying the gloomy girl that was suddenly framed in the glass.

She tried to look away, but I forced myself to meet my own eyes.

"Celeste was waiting at the restroom door for *you* to have the guts to walk down the hall with her inside that forcefield." The loose feeling of queasiness I'd felt all afternoon instantly became a hard ball of pain in my stomach. "And you *knew* it, and she *knew* that you knew it."

CHAPTER 12

Just because I was disgusted by something awful and cowardly I'd done didn't mean I was brave enough not to do it again. I woke up Friday morning longing to explain to Celeste and apologize for not walking with her. But the price of walking with her today might be some kind of run-in with Tricia and her friends and I just couldn't handle that, especially not on Luau Day.

So I put myself in zombie-mode. After choir, I avoided both Celeste and Tricia's bunch by not making my usual stop in the restroom. And other times that day when I could have crossed the hall to chat with Celeste or at least waved from across a classroom, I pretended I was busy looking through my books.

At the same time, I illogically hoped that Celeste would ignore the fact that I was ignoring *her* and smile that genuine smile in my direction again.

But in yearbook class, she caught me staring at her back and gave me a quick, cool, high-chinned look from behind that beautiful mask of hers. My stomach plummeted like I'd just been pushed from a helicopter.

By the end of school that day, my heart actually hurt. I tried to chalk it up to the ravioli we'd had in the cafeteria at lunch.

On some deep level, though, I must have known the real reason, because as Nancy, Kelly, Margot and I worked frantically on my patio that afternoon, I couldn't concentrate at all. All I could think about was this sudden overwhelming need I had for Celeste to show up at the luau.

"Don't you think there's a chance Celeste will decide to come tonight after all?"

Nancy and Margot were balancing the palm trees along the fence, and Kelly and I had just finished stacking volcanic rocks in piles. The patio was littered with rotting mimosa blossoms, but they looked so much like dead jellyfish that we'd decided to leave them and call them that.

"You've asked us that about a dozen times, Frannie," Nancy snapped, fluffing out some palm leaves that had partly dissolved in yesterday's rain. "I wish you'd just quit stewing about it. *You're* the one who told us she said not to worry, that she wouldn't be coming. So relax—she won't be!"

Finally, at about 5:30, they all went home, Kelly to decorate Nibbles and Margot and Nancy to do the luau cooking. They were all coming back in a couple of hours.

"Mom?" I called, slouching into the house. "Did a girl named Celeste call while I was outside?"

"I'm working on Mitch," Mom called back, and I followed her voice to the bathroom, where she was trying to get a comb through Mitch's crazy hair. Mom and Dad had agreed to take the boys out for pizza while the luau was getting underway.

"You did get a phone call just now," Mom said.

"Celeste?" I asked eagerly.

"No, it was Nancy. She said her mother doesn't want the mess in her kitchen, so she's coming back over here to do the food in *our* kitchen. She's on her way."

Mom raised her right eyebrow but smiled slightly to tell me she knew how Nancy was so she wasn't going to make a big deal out of it.

"Thank you," I said, and hugged her. I didn't let go right away, even though Mitch was jabbing me in the ribs with his pointy elbow, trying to get me to.

Nancy used every pan in our kitchen to prepare three sacks of corn chips and two bowls of canned bean dip.

"I thought this kind of food was Mexican," I mentioned listlessly.

"Mexican cuisine was inspired by Hawaiian cuisine,"

Nancy said, a fact I was pretty sure she'd just made up that second.

Next, she used all Mom's long spoons and measuring cups and four pitchers to make red Kool-aid. She dumped it into the huge aluminum bowl we usually put popcorn in on Sunday nights. Little oil slicks rose to the surface as I staggered out to the patio with it.

Kelly rode up. Nibbles had a fluffy gold garland wrapped around her middle several times and two green and red plastic Christmas wreaths draped over her ears like a set of incredibly tacky hoop earrings.

Margot arrived, put a big plate of tiny sandwiches with pinkish stuff peeking out of them on one of the two food tables, and hustled into the kitchen.

"You guys better come out here—everybody's going to be arriving any minute!" I yelled at her and Nancy through the kitchen window.

"You and Kelly will be the greeters," Nancy yelled back, fanning her face with her apron. Yes, she'd actually brought along an apron. "Margot and I are staying in here until the party's underway, to replenish the food."

Dumbfounded, I looked helplessly up at Kelly. She and Nibbles were still parked in the patio entrance like a big, gaudy statue.

"They're hiding," she said, stating the obvious, as usual. "They don't want to have to get people to mingle and stuff, especially the boys."

"Well who *does?*" I moaned. I spotted the moon, which had fallen into the grass behind the water spigot and gotten all soggy and lumpy. I walked over, picked it up, and slouched against the fence, aimlessly peeling layers off it, trying to get a grip on the awful feeling of impending doom that was filling me like mud.

Right about then, Max, Jason and Theodore C. Rockman arrived in the go-cart and chugged right onto the patio. All my anguished instructions had obviously slipped their minds. They began happily doing wheelies, taking up every inch of room and making Nibbles bare her teeth. Though Kelly reined her in hard, she reared up in anger, flipping her earrings backward into the Kool-aid.

"Mad horse! Run for your lives!" Jason shrieked as he plowed the go-cart right into one of the two food tables, collapsing its front legs. Margot's little tuna fish sandwiches slid upside down into Max's lap, and the impact started an avalanche of the volcanic rocks we'd piled around the bottom.

All those bouncing boulders panicked Nibbles. She galloped into the yard and began whirling in circles, chasing a little piece of gold tinsel that dangled from her stomach while Kelly held on for dear life.

Right about then, most of the eighth grade boys arrived.

"Hey, cool!" Skip Rethman yelled, pointing to the sandwiches sticking to Max. "Food fight, everybody!"

Things became a blur of legs and hooting and flying sandwiches and boulders, then someone kicked some of the boulders into the yard. Most of the action had moved out there by the time the girls started arriving, so they sort of clumped themselves in a semi-circle around the tangle of boys and stood swatting the gnats that zeroed in on their ankles.

Celeste was nowhere to be seen, which, though I'd expected it, somehow seemed like the awfullest thing of all.

I forced myself to walk over to the girls in the yard. "You guys want to come to the patio and get something to eat? Or . . . drink? It's less . . . buggy on the patio."

Please, please, God! Make them think those circles of flowers in the punch are floating decorations, and not earrings that were just on a horse!

"Haven't you got chairs or anything for us to sit on out here?" Sally Myers asked.

I swallowed. "Not really," I answered. "Want some Hawaiian bean dip and corn chips?"

"Are the boys *staying* out here in your yard?" Carla asked. "Because what're they *doing* out there, anyhow?"

The boys had kicked the rocks to shreds and were now using the palm trees to pummel each other. I cleared my throat. "It's a Hawaiian party game. Palm boxing, it's called."

"I didn't know this was going to be a sports party,"

Tricia Harmon said, rolling her eyes. "I thought we'd, like, dance or *some*thing."

"Hey, I just remembered!" I was surprised my brain hadn't completely petrified with humiliation. "I'll be right back. We've got some chairs in the garage."

When I got a few yards from them, I ducked behind our juniper hedge, then began running in the opposite direction of the garage toward the alley. It was pretty dark now. No one seemed to notice that I was sneaking away. Hunched like an animal, I crossed the alley, then looked back. Most of the girls were still swatting and posing for the boys. A few of them were walking toward the patio. No one was even looking in my direction.

I don't think I hesitated at all, then, before running into the field, which shows you how desperate I was. The Quiver Serpent didn't even enter my mind. I knew only one thing—I had to get to the platform in the rocket ship, where no one would find me and I could think up a plan. Maybe I could somehow contact Mitch or Harley and bribe them to bring food to me up there a couple of times a week. Maybe they'd bring me a sleeping bag.

"Rah-ah-ah-ah-bin!" I sobbed as I ran. "Robin, where are you when I need you so, so desperately? I gave my whole heart and soul to this party, Robin, and as you see, it's the worst disaster in the world and no one is making a move to accept their one-fourth of the blame! Rah-ah-bin!"

Choking and stumbling, I finally reached the ladder, slumped down on the bottom rung, and began giving myself a big sob-studded lecture.

"Oh, you think you're so cuh-cuh-*cool,* Frannie S. Driscoll, now don't you? You didn't even have chuh-chuh-chairs! Call yourself a singer? Half the class was on the good singers list! Your bangs curve the wrong way, you buh-buh-bite your nails, and you're scared to *move!* Call yourself a *woman?* Ha! You're nothing but a pet-starving child who gives parties that are restricted or segregated or whatever the stupid right word is."

Suddenly, the ladder moved.

I jumped up, terrified right out of my hysterics. The *serpent!*

"Frannie?" Celeste asked softly from the darkness over my head. "You okay?"

CHAPTER 13

She was lying on her stomach, just like I'd been the night I'd spied on her from up there on the rocket platform. The blue velvet of twilight framed her face and shoulders.

"Celeste!"

"Come up," she whisper-called.

Someone back in my yard began screaming the kind of ear-splitting scream you only hear in disaster movies. Celeste bounced to her knees and strained forward through the bars, trying to hear what was happening. I scrambled up the ladder and knelt beside her and listened, too, but I couldn't make myself care all that much. I was feeling too light-headed with relief. "What are you *doing* up here, Celeste? I didn't think you were coming!"

A very distinct, very angry voice reached us from across the dark field then.

"It was *not* a party decoration, Theodore, and you *know* it! Don't lie to me! You put a real lizard in my sandwich, and I almost bit right *in*to it! I could have *swallowed* it!"

"Whoever that girl is, her voice certainly does carry," Celeste murmured, sounding impressed and horrified at once.

"That happens to be Tricia, and you and I both know she's got the biggest mouth in the history of the world!" I chirped. I think I was hoping a super-blast of snottiness about Tricia would make Celeste forget how snotty I'd acted to *her* at school today.

Tricia's original scream started a mini-fad, and a bunch of people back in my yard began screaming fake screams as they hurried from the yard in shadowy groups.

"Well, party's over." I dropped to my bottom on the splintery platform and shoved with my heels until I felt the bars on the far side hit my back. "I'm usually pretty good at imagining the worst, but even *I* didn't think this would turn out so awful."

Suddenly, I just couldn't keep from grinning. "I'm just so, so glad *you* decided to show up, Celeste."

Celeste turned toward me, biting her bottom lip. "Uh, Frannie, I've been climbing up into this rocket every night this week to practice my singing."

So she hadn't been coming to the luau after all. "Oh," I pushed out.

"I *would* have been at the party," she said slowly, "but, well, it was obvious from how you acted today that you didn't really—"

Don't let her finish that sentence!

"You know what?" I interrupted, blathering. "I just figured out what that lizard sandwich stuff was about. See, my pet salamander, Janice, was in a coffee can under the table on the patio! Theodore must have put her on Tricia's plate. He can't stand her."

Celeste looked off-balance. "Theodore can't stand your . . . salamander?"

"No, my salamander is dead. Theodore can't stand Tricia because she's always asking stupid questions in class just to impress the teachers and to get the cute boys to look at her."

Celeste nodded. "We had Natalie who did that in St. Louis. So . . . why do you keep your dead salamander in a can on your patio?"

"It's just temporary. I'm going to bury her. It seems like I owe her a nice burial in a shoebox instead of just being dropped into the dumpster in that gloppy can."

"Why do you say you 'owe' her more? Because she was your pet?"

I took a deep breath. "No. Because . . . I . . . I sort of accidentally starved her."

"That's awful!" Celeste cried.

I cringed. "I was a little afraid of her, so I guess I just

99

sort of put her out of my mind and left her there in the corner of the basement until . . . "

". . . too late," Celeste finished for me. "Why'd you get her in the first place if you didn't want to take care of her?"

I sighed. "My grandpa found her in the mud out in his pig pen. I was afraid I'd hurt his feelings by not taking her. He was so happy about giving me something."

At first she didn't say anything. Then she murmured, "I don't guess *Janice* feels any too happy right now."

I tilted back my head. A stinging feeling was starting behind my eyes, so I focused hard on the Big Dipper, which was hanging in the black sky like God's big glowing box kite.

"I've been weird every time I've been with you this week," I pushed out. "But you probably figured that out already."

"With me, you're afraid of what people *think,* like you said in the restroom yesterday."

With me. She thought I was treating her as lousy as I'd treated poor Janice.

The Big Dipper jiggled and blurred. I forced out a painful, "I'm sorry."

"Frannie?" Celeste whispered after a minute. "You've got to decide. It's not going to get any easier. I think we've got a lot in common, but compared to being my girlfriend at a school like Quiver Junior, feeding the

ugliest and most bad-tempered of flesh-eating salaman-
ders would be nothing."

"I know that," I whispered back. "But what choice do
I have?"

"Oh, right." Celeste shook her head and sounded
hurt. "I forgot. You don't want people thinking you have
me as a friend, so you *have* no choice."

"No!" In panic, I scooted toward her. "I meant, I have
no choice about *wanting* to be your friend! I don't want
to spend my life telling . . . telling palm boxing lies to
people I don't even respect. I can really talk to you Celeste, and I just *like* you. And I want with all my heart
to promise you I'll never wimp out again, but I may be
too wimpy to keep that promise. All I can do is promise
to *try* not to keep wimping out. So I guess that means
you're the one who has a choice to make." I took a deep
breath, dreading her answer. "Am I worth the trouble it
would take to be *my* friend?"

For a long time she looked across at me in the darkness, frowning slightly.

She *did* think I was too much trouble. Too wishy-
washy and weak, too untrustworthy. My chest felt
squeezed, and tears burned my esophagus.

"I came up here and sang one night, too," I confessed
in a miserable whisper. "I pretended Dick Clark was at
my side, raving into his microphone about how *good* I
was. What a laugh. I'm always doing that, imagining a

cheering section, whether it's skating or sculpting or singing. Pretty pathetic, huh?"

But Celeste quickly leaned toward me. "That's *it!* *Prove* you can choose not to be afraid to do something risky in front of *real* people, Frannie. Audition Tuesday for the girls' double trio. We'll go together and both audition, even though those girls don't want me."

"No! Oh, no, I can't. I *can't!* I mean, I'm not nearly good enough."

"How can you be so sure of that? You don't need to hide behind any old imaginary Dick Clark! Tell yourself you've got a shot. That's what teaches you courage, Frannie. Telling yourself over and over every single day that you've got a shot, whether you're afraid to think that or not."

My head was shaking side to side—*no, no, no!* "I can think of ten, maybe twelve girls in chorus who sing better than me! I was probably about the last person she picked for the good singers list, and even if I did make the cut, which I wouldn't, I'd probably screw up at competition or something and everybody would blame . . . "

I caught my breath and covered my mouth with my hands.

Celeste nodded her head, smiling. Then very quietly she said, "Prove you can choose not to be afraid of this one thing, Frannie. Prove it. To you *and* me." She crossed her arms.

I put my face in my hands, then split apart my fingers and smiled sheepishly from behind them. "All right, all right! I'll try out! I'll make a complete fool of myself, but I'll try out!"

"You won't make a fool of yourself, silly," she said, smiling back at me.

And then, I guess we both felt shy. We quickly looked away from each other and up at the stars, which were staring down at us like bright-eyed animals. For a second or two, I imagined we were floating upwards to become a constellation ourselves.

"You out there someplace, Frannie?" Kelly suddenly called. Nibbles' accompanying neigh sounded like it came from deep space. "Everybody's looking for you. Call back if you're out there."

Guiltily, I scrambled to my knees and made my hands into a megaphone. "Up here, Kell! In the rocket! I'll be there in just a sec!"

"That's Kelly, right?" Celeste asked. "The tall, quiet girl with almost-white hair?"

I nodded. "She's a cowgirl. You'll like her."

"Fran-*nie?* C'est la vou? Le *vou,* mon cheri, instantly em-*wah!*"

"And that's Margot," I told Celeste. "She fakes French to be glamorous. Besides her doing that, we're all totally . . . unglamorous. Ordinary, I mean."

"Frannie, come back to your yard this minute and help clean up!"

"And that's Nancy," I explained. "Our other friend. Her goal is to be the entire world's most ladylike of mothers. Will you come back with me, to meet them?"

"Wait," Celeste said.

She had two rhinestone-covered bobby pins holding back her hair, and she took one out and held it up between us. The moonlight made the rhinestones flash like fire.

"Star sisters?" she whispered.

At that moment, my heart just sort of leaped. I think it—my heart, I mean—understood right away that Celeste was the heart-friend I'd longed for all my life. My brain only completely understood that later, when it seemed too late.

I took the bobby pin and solemnly worked it into my own tangled hair.

"Star sisters," I whispered back.

CHAPTER 14

Look who I found!" I called out when Celeste and I got close enough to see two shapes together in the alley and another on a horse swishing through the weeds at the field's edge. I began skipping and jumping, sailing up and over the tall weeds like a dolphin. I ran back to grab Celeste's wrist and drag her along. "I brought Celeste! I found Celeste and brought her, you guys!"

Nibbles whinnied and Celeste broke free of my grip and hurried over to rub her nose. Nibbles closed her eyes and lowered her head as Celeste crooned to her and moved both hands in wide, gentle circles over her forehead and around her ears.

"You speak her language," Kelly said, sliding to the ground. "You must ride."

"I don't have my own horse," Celeste whispered. "There's a stable near our house in St. Louis where you can rent horses, though, and I get to ride there sometimes on weekends."

Nancy bounced on her heels, impatient with the horse talk and energized by the chance to expose a new guest to the previously doomed party. "Well, I'm practically sure there's still plenty of dip!" she exclaimed. "Let's all join the others back on the patio, shall we?"

Kelly let Celeste have the reins to lead Nibbles back through the dark, plaster-littered yard. As we maneuvered around the broken palm trees, Margot hung back from the rest of us and supplied a commentary of the party devastation in peevish-sounding fake French. "C'est le vie! Le torn up decora-she-*uns!* Le smasheroony! Le mess, mess, mess!"

"Quel disastre," Celeste agreed, turning around to her and nodding sadly.

Margot looked pop-eyed with surprise, then smiled a self-satisfied smile and took a little hop over to walk by Celeste's left side.

I brought up the rear, feeling, to tell the truth, a little abandoned.

When we reached the light of the patio, "the others" Nancy'd mentioned turned out to be Theodore, Jason and Max, just as I thought they would be. They were still under the caved-in table playing chess.

Theodore looked up when we approached. "You should know, Frannie, that I attempted to supply one of your guests with a small party favor and she was extremely unappreciative. My apologies for any confusion caused."

"A small, mummified amphibian that apparently had once existed in the hydrangea border but had then crept into an old can and died there," Max mumbled, looking down at the chessboard and stroking his chin. He pushed a rook toward one of Jason's pawns.

"Punch?" Nancy asked, holding the still-full bowl of oily Kool-aid out to Celeste.

"I'm not too thirsty right now, thanks, but your dip looks delicious," Celeste said.

She had to be kidding! At this point, Nancy's dip looked like dried mud!

But Celeste loaded up a corn chip with a big, hard chunk of it then crouched down next to Jason, munching and studying the game.

Theodore peered at her over his glasses. "You play?"

Celeste shrugged. "A little."

"Oh no, you don't, Theodore! She's not going to play, she's going to *eat!*" growled Nancy.

Now that the awful party frenzy was over and everyone had more or less returned to their senses, it was easy to see that they'd all take to Celeste. But looking at *them* through a stranger's eyes, through *her* eyes, they suddenly seemed to me to be so . . . so peculiar. Would *she* take to *them?*

Nancy was still wearing that white lace apron with the yellow daisies. Margot was posed in her most sophisticated French way, with one hip cocked and her chin thrust out—*but* she had a piece of palm tree sticking up from her permanent like a TV antenna. The go-cart was still where it had crashed, and Nibbles had accidentally straddled it somehow and now couldn't move forward or backward. Kelly was trying to coax her sideways with a hardened chunk of dip. Jason had retrieved Nibbles' earrings from the Kool-aid and for some reason was wearing them around his own ears. Theodore and Max looked like spies, with their white shirts and black-rimmed glasses and briefcases.

I mumbled something about getting some trash bags and pulled Celeste into the kitchen. "Don't drink the punch!" I warned her. "It's had horse earrings in it. And . . . how do you like my friends?"

I braced myself.

"I thought you said they were ordinary," she answered, grinning. "My father the professor would say they're a collection of very unique and interesting individuals."

It's hard to imagine, but if it hadn't been for Celeste, I might have gone on thinking of them as ordinary forever.

"They sure like *you.* They probably like you better than me, in fact," I said, trying not to sound like my feelings were hurt. "French, horse-riding, chess—is there anything you *don't* do well?"

She looked at me in a puzzled way, then laughed. "I don't do *any* of that stuff well, Frannie. I love horses but don't get to ride all that often. My dad taught me chess when I was just a little kid, but I'm just barely average at it."

I squinted my eyes suspiciously. "What about the French?"

"I took one semester last year." She folded her arms and took a deep breath. "It's a trick, Frannie. When I'm trying to fit in with people, especially white kids? I just sort of figure out what they're interested in and find a way to relate to it. I've felt so lonely here in Quiver that maybe I, well, laid it on a little thick tonight."

I thought about that. "Not really. Well, okay, eating Nancy's dip might have been a teeny bit overboard." I smiled.

Her eyes flashed. "The only thing I truly want to do well is sing," she said.

After everything was pretty well cleaned up and the others went home, Celeste stayed for a few minutes to help me sort through the trash bags for Janice, who'd gotten thrown away with Tricia's plate. We found her stuck to a big glob of somebody's gum.

"I *will* bury you this weekend, before anything else happens," I promised as I peeled her off.

Celeste raised her arms over her head and stretched. "Will you call me tomorrow about practicing for tryouts?"

"Sure," I said. "We could practice here, except my little brothers will drive us crazy."

"We could practice at my house," she said, "if you're not afraid of the spooks."

"So, you heard about your house being used as a spook house last Hallowe'en, huh?" I laughed a small, tired laugh as I bent to put Janice back in her can. "We used to think the field where we were tonight was haunted, too. There was supposed to be a monster snake prowling around under it."

Behind me, Celeste said, quietly, "Uh, Frannie, I haven't heard any stories about my house."

Invisible fingers brushed the back of my neck, making me shiver as I nudged the can under the table with my toe. "Then why'd you mention . . . spooks?"

"Okay, please don't talk about this in front of my dad. And don't ask me anything, because I can't answer, at least not yet. But, well, my house *is* haunted. That's why Dad bought it. He's writing a book about it, and . . . other things here in Quiver. The field is haunted, too. Worse than you probably think."

"Cut it out!" I was probably supposed to laugh, so I forced a snicker.

Celeste had taken a couple of sleepwalkerlike steps into the yard and was looking toward the field. "Sorry," she said, turning to face me, "what did you say?"

I gulped. "I just said, quit kidding around," I whispered hoarsely.

But she wasn't kidding around. The look on her face told me that beyond the shadow of a doubt.

CHAPTER 15

I managed to get to my room and into bed that night without running into my parents, but Mom was full of eager questions at breakfast Saturday morning.

"So, come on, Fran. Tell us how the big party went last night!"

"Fine," I said, shaking my hair out of my eyes and helping myself to the scrambled eggs. "Uh, Mom? Where are the boys?"

"Still asleep. Your father and I weren't being nosy, but we didn't see too many people around when we got home from pizza last night. Short, uncrowded parties are sometimes the most fun, though. Right?"

"Right, Mom. Uh, Daddy? Remember about a week ago when we were discussing the old Teschler house? You said it was a strange old place. What'd you mean by that? I mean *exactly* what'd you mean?"

He lowered his paper and frowned. "I said that?"

"Did you mean strange about the old house itself or strange about Mr. Teschler? Because I sort of remember Mr. Teschler. He used to be sitting in his undershirt on the porch steps of that house with a cigar in his mouth when my friends and I rode by on our bikes on the way to the pool. He'd always be clutching this big old stick, like a broomstick or something, I think it was. He held it between his hands like he was going to brain some-body with it. And he had all those weird signs sticking up from his yard telling people to keep away and stay off his grass. He never even had any grass that I could see. He'd glare at us, and kids said he killed cats sometimes just because they couldn't read and came into his yard."

"What's the party last night got to do with Norman Teschler?" Daddy asked.

"Nothing," I said, shrugging. "But how'd Mr. Teschler die? People at school say his heart exploded and jet black blood spurted out of his ears. Some people say he caught on fire right there on his porch. Spontaneous com-bustion, they call it. It only happens to truly evil people."

"Frannie!"

"It's okay, Mom, the boys aren't out here, remem-ber?" I turned back to Daddy. "He worked at your fac-tory, didn't he? So you must have known him a little. *Was* he truly evil? Some kids at school say he conducted Satanic rituals in the attic of that house, which is why he had those trash bags taped over the upstairs windows. Some people think he killed the cats to use them in those rituals, too. Do you know if that's true? Because some kids think that's why the house is haunted, those rituals, which are keeping his evil spirit alive up there. In that attic, I mean."

I was talking awfully fast, and my heart was racing, and I knew they were both shocked, to say the least. But I had to clear this up if I could. Celeste was actually *living* in that house, and she had some reason to think that those silly old stories weren't silly at all. *My house is haunted.* Those had been her exact words.

Daddy leaned toward me on his elbows. "Frannie, listen. Norman Teschler was just an angry, lonely man. He drank too much and his heart gave out." He looked at Mom quickly, then looked back at me. "Your mother might not approve of me telling you this, but apparently Norman had some kind of secret parties going on up in that attic upon occasion. That was the talk at work. People coming to his place late at night, most from out of town. Probably just some kind of gambling, lots of liquor. That was the reason for blacking out those windows, nothing more sinister."

I swallowed. "That house looks like a skull with those two blacked-out upstairs windows. They look like eyeless sockets. There's a feeling about that place. Some kids say—"

Mom slapped both hands down on the table. "Fran, that is enough! You've always been too smart to believe that kind of malarky! What in the world has gotten into you?"

I drank my juice in several fast gulps, trying to swallow down the rest of my questions.

"Is it okay if I go to a friend's house this afternoon?" I asked when I'd finished.

Mom looked confused for a second and then relieved by the topic change. But she said, "Don't you remember, Frannie? I asked you to sit for the boys this afternoon while your dad and I drive out to Great Aunt Lena's to help her give her cats their flea protection pills. It may take a while. She'll probably get out the old family photo albums of your father when he was a little boy."

"Why's she have such big old headstrong cats, anyhow?" I complained, but weakly.

I knew Aunt Lena needed company, and I *had* told Mom I'd babysit.

And besides, talking about Mr. Teschler and repeating all those old rumors about his house had given me the creeps, and I wasn't so sure I really *wanted* to go over there today after all.

Everybody ended up coming to my house instead. On a different Saturday afternoon, Margot and Nancy and even Kelly might have griped about having to sprawl on the kitchen floor and color in old coloring books with Mitch and Harley, but that day everyone actually seemed to enjoy it. I guess we were all exhausted from the effort of planning the luau, then trying to ignore the fact that it had been a disaster. I doubt if Celeste would have griped. I have a strong suspicion that, like me, she was a closet crayon fanatic.

"See," Celeste said, tilting her Spring Fantasies coloring book toward Harley, "this garden is like ones they have on Saturn, where it's cold and icy. These are icedrop petunias and snowflower trees. That's Queen Frigidaire in the background, sitting on her ice-mountain throne."

"Oh," Harley breathed, his eyes round with wonder.

"Lemme see that!" Mitch jumped up and came to crouch with one foot partly on Celeste's book. "That picture's just a bunch of yellow and blue flowers." He jabbed the book with a grubby, accusing finger. "You *drew* that mountain and that girl there!"

"You can draw things in coloring books," Kelly informed him.

Mitch instantly shut up and went back to his spot on the floor. He always believed anything Kelly said. She was the only person in the world that impressed him.

"Want to see me draw a flying elephant?" Celeste asked Mitch.

He shook his head vigorously. He was lying on his

stomach between Nancy and Margot, propped with his coloring book between his elbows. He didn't look up at Celeste, but just kept staring hard at the race car he was obliterating with layers of heavy black crayon.

Harley, meanwhile, snuggled as close to Celeste as he could, mesmerized by her coloring talent and by the polite way she spoke to him like he was a real person instead of somebody's pesky little brother.

"Quit being rude, Mitch," I said. "Why are you so grouchy today, anyhow?"

"How about a flying elephant that looks exactly like Dumbo?" Celeste coaxed.

Mitch slammed his book shut, folded his arms across it and thunked his forehead down on them. "I'm not *listening* to her when she talks! She's got the wrong *skin* on!"

Harley went on coloring, humming softly to himself, but an electric current sizzled though the rest of us, freezing and burning at once. No one knew what to say. Nancy's neck turned bright pink, and Margot covered her mouth with her hands and closed her eyes. Kelly glared across at Mitch like she would have liked to lasso him and tie him to a cactus. I would gladly have supplied her with the rope.

"Mitch?" Celeste said softly. "Come on over here and touch my arm, okay?"

Mitch shook his head, not lifting his face.

"I think she's got *pretty* skin on," Harley said, caressing Celeste's arm.

Celeste smiled at that. "Thanks, Harley. I happen to like it just fine, too."

Mitch got up and ran out of the kitchen, kicking a chair leg on his way. I jumped to my feet to go after him, so furious I was close to tears.

But Celeste grabbed my ankle. "Let him be, Frannie. Please?"

I hesitated, rolling my eyes to show my disagreement, then reluctantly sat back down.

Celeste put her chin in her hands and sighed. "He's just got a bunch of questions in his head. Why wouldn't he? The stores are full of blonde, blue-eyed Barbies and Kens. The only colored kid I've seen on Saturday morning TV is that Buckwheat character on *The Little Rascals,* the one with the wild hair that's supposed to be funny because he acts stupid. And here's one that really gets me—have you ever seen a brown-skinned angel in any of the pictures in your Bibles?"

I could see Nancy frowning in concentration, trying desperately to remember one. "Where's your Bible, Frannie?" she finally asked, and when I told her, she jumped up to go get it from my room.

Celeste chuckled. "My father the professor says the white viewpoint in America is 'all-pervasive' and that leaves minorities 'marginalized.' He's always using words like that. What he means is that every bread wrapper and laundry commercial and car advertisement features cute white kids with their smiling white mothers and fathers."

Margot guiltily chewed her lip. "We were all sort of scared of you at first, Celeste, mon cheri. We were afraid we wouldn't know what to talk to you about."

I was still so angry at Mitch that I didn't trust my voice, so I began quietly gathering some of the scattered crayons while the others talked. My eyes lit on the label of one of the beige ones—it read *flesh*. There were two browns and a yellow rolling around near my knee, and I nudged them up and read their labels—*brown, dark brown, yellow.*

Nancy reappeared, her nose in my red Bible. "Sure enough, the angels look like blonde Barbie dolls—*skinny* blonde Barbies. Noah looks like Benjamin Franklin, only not bald on top. Jesus Christ looks a little like Elvis Presley, now that I notice it, only with longer hair and without the guitar."

Celeste and I met up in the rocket Sunday night to finally practice for tryouts. We sang through a few songs in our chorus books, then we sank to our stomachs, propped ourselves on our elbows, and just silently watched the highway lights.

After a while, Celeste looked off to the left and

pointed where I'd seen her and her father pick up that crusty black thing. Had it really been only one week ago tonight?

"Frannie, do you see anything over that way, in the weeds? Look closely."

My heartbeat got a little faster, though when I leaned in that direction and tried with all my might to see something, I saw nothing. "What am I looking for, exactly?" I whispered.

"A dark shape, like a shadow. Several feet long."

I shook my head. All I saw was a blowing ocean of weeds. Under those weeds I knew there was broken glass, burned metal, all sorts of decaying, hidden stuff.

I cleared my throat and took a deep breath. "Celeste, I have to tell you something. I . . . spied on you out here. I saw you with your dad. I was up here, lying on my stomach just like we are now. It was that Dick Clark night, and you two just suddenly appeared so I hit the deck and . . . watched."

She just looked at me. I could see moving headlights reflected in her clear eyes.

"I heard your father say the field was blighted and cursed. And . . . soaked in blood. Are we looking for bloodstains out there in the weeds, Celeste?"

The wind gusted and the weeds beneath us blew and thrashed, as though trying to tell us something.

Celeste shook her head. "Not blood," she whispered.

"There's plenty of *that* soaked in deep down there, too, but do you . . . *feel* anything strange when you look out there?"

I swallowed. "I always get a creepy feeling about the field, like it's just sort of . . . off. Not right. Not quite belonging in this dimension. Uh, Celeste? One other thing about that night I watched you and your father. You found something. I mean, if it's secret, that's okay, you don't have to tell me. But I've been curious about what it was."

Curious—what an understatement! I braced myself, expecting to be horrified.

She smiled and shrugged. "It was a harmonica, Frannie. A really old one. It's been burned and to most people it would look like a regular old charred stick with some metal melted to it, but my father's pretty sure it's a harmonica. We found a few buttons that night, too." She jumped to her feet. "Come on, we've *got* to practice."

A harmonica? *That* was the burned fingery thing they'd held and explored so carefully? That was what made her father talk about curses and blights and blood stains?

We practiced for an hour or so longer, then walked back through the field together.

"By the way," I told her, "I don't care what you say, I *am* going to have a little talk with Mitch about his rudeness to you yesterday."

After a minute, she said, "If you come down hard on him, he'll probably just get more stubborn about it. I want him to like me, Frannie. If he has a chance to get to know me, he'll get over being afraid."

We walked in silence then, and said good-bye when we got to the edge of the field. I crossed the alley and stood under the streetlight, watching her walk the first of the seven blocks to her house. She felt my eyes, and turned to walk backwards.

"Really, Frannie, don't be hard on Mitch!" she called, her hands a megaphone. "I'll keep trying to win his confidence. Dr. King says peaceful resistance is the only way to open a closed mind and calm a fearful heart!"

I nodded and waved, figuring Dr. King must be her family physician back in St. Louis.

CHAPTER 16

Kelly, Margot, Nancy, Celeste and I met in front of the school Monday morning so we could walk in together. The other four of us planned to stay close to Celeste all day in hopes that the forcefield around her would stretch to its limit with five people inside and finally pop. We also hoped we wouldn't feel so humiliated about the luau if most of us were there to shrug it off whenever anyone made a wisecrack about it.

We survived the whispers and rolled eyes and cracks that day. Once in the hall someone threw a couple of paper wads at us, but that didn't, of course, hurt. The words were what hurt. When the final bell rang, we were all relieved that the day was over. Tomorrow, when anyone told a luau joke, we could laugh back at them and say it was ancient history and why didn't they quit being square and come into the twentieth century?

And tomorrow, people would surely be a tiny bit more used to Celeste being our friend and us being hers.

Our guard was down as we hustled toward the concrete steps in front of the building that afternoon, talking and laughing. Then suddenly, this kid named Randy Javits detached himself from the group of guys he'd been with and came running up the stairs at us, holding his arms out like scrawny airplane wings.

"Go back to the jungle where you done come from!" he yelled at Celeste, then arced back down to his whooping bunch of friends, who had probably dared him to fly up and deliver that hilarious remark.

We all stopped walking and just stood there, stunned. Kelly put her hands on her hips and took a slow, deliberate step down toward Randy and his friends. They all looked up at her uneasily, and you could see their laughter becoming forced. Some of them looked poised to run.

But then *Nancy* stepped down next to Kelly and thrust one jiggling pink arm across Kelly's chest to stop her from going any farther.

"Let *me* handle this," she ordered, and before Kelly could argue, Nancy began mincing down the last three steps.

My heart sank as I watched the boys begin to snicker and punch each other again. If they thought *this* was funny, wait till they heard Nancy deliver her "you don't sound very Christian" lecture while wagging one index finger in their faces.

By the time Nancy pulled up even with them, they were doubled over with laughter. This made it easy for her to reach out and grab Randy's left ear lobe between the long nails of her thumb and forefinger. She didn't say a word, just held his ear, pinching.

It didn't take him long to break. "Oooooowwwww! Stop, you're killing me!"

"You know what to say, so please just say it," Nancy calmly requested.

"Let him go! You heard him—you're killin' the guy!" his friends pleaded, grimacing and covering their own ears with their hands.

Randy fell to his knees, writhing and groaning.

"I can do this forever," Nancy explained, smiling patiently. "I drink orange-flavored gelatin every day for strong nails."

"Help me, you guys!" Randy screeched to his friends.

But they had backed away, and were cowering out of reach. Nancy had *another* set of Parfait Pink weapons, after all.

"Say it," Nancy suggested. "Simply tell Celeste you're sorry."

"I'm *sorry!*" Randy finally howled. "I'm *sah*-ree!! I'm *reeeeally* sorry. I am *sorry!*"

Nancy let him go. "Now please don't let it happen

again. I would hate to report you to Principal Winger, since I know you hoods are basically on permanent probation."

She turned and minced in a high-chinned ladylike way back up the stairs to us.

We managed to keep our composure till we were a block away, then Kelly, Margot, Celeste and I dropped our books and collapsed in the grass. We clutched our stomachs and laughed till we were nearly sick, but all that time Nancy just stood there on the sidewalk looking totally bewildered.

"I just can't imagine what came over me," she kept saying. "I just wasn't very . . . *nice!*"

"You were great, Nancy," Kelly corrected her.

"Oui, mon cheri," Margot added, "And Randy's a big baby. You squeezed *our* ears harder than that before you pierced them last year, and *we* hardly screamed at all."

Celeste and I had our last practice before tryouts up in the rocket that night. I could get all the words and notes right, but I sounded so *plain* compared to her.

"You make people *feel* things when you sing," I told her. "How do you *do* that?"

She laughed. "Thanks. That's a great compliment. My chorus teacher in St. Louis told us to sing with passion. I just try to slip inside the skin of whatever character is supposed to be singing the song, then I sing it like she would sing it. It could be a shepherdess, or a queen, or, like in *Oklahoma,* a pioneer homesteader in love with a cowboy." She sighed and hugged herself. "Oh, Frannie, for my birthday last year my parents took me to New York City, where I heard Miss Leontyne Price sing at the Metropolitan Opera. It was the first time I had heard anyone sing like that, and it was the most wonderful experience of my life."

Celeste closed her eyes and began softly singing something she later told me was an aria from *Madame Butterfly.* She said it was "simplified" from the original, but it sure didn't sound simple to me. The Italian words and the complicated runs were as far above my head as the stars were, and I was breathless, watching her lift her eyes and then her arms longingly to the heavens. She was every heroine who had ever felt wonderful, sad things under a lonely night sky.

"My dream is to sing opera someday," she told me, plopping back down cross-legged before the last beautiful note had faded away. She stuck the gob of gum she'd had waiting on its wrapper back into her mouth.

"Don't *do* that!" I complained.

"Do what?" she asked, innocently licking her gummy fingers.

"Don't break the mood like that!" I was surprised to find that I was really, truly mad at her. "Why'd you have to just . . . just *thud* us back down to reality? Tomorrow's going to be hard, so why couldn't we just . . ."

"Avoid it? Stay here in the stars? Become full-time opera heroines?" She giggled. "Frannie, you're something else, girl, you know that?"

There was a big lump in my throat, leftover from the song, but growing. "I'm afraid, Celeste," I pushed out. "What if I . . . fail you tomorrow? We got through today, but we were all five together most of the time and still it was hard. Tomorrow, in tryouts, you and I will be there alone, with mostly just Tricia's crowd. What if . . ."

"What if *what?* You won't let me down, Frannie. If everyone laughs, or tries to goof me up, you won't. I know that, so *you* know it, too, okay? I'll be there for you, and you for me. We'll pretend we're singing up here, in our starplace. Nothing will stop us, okay?"

I nodded. I couldn't talk around the lump now, but I nodded as hard as I could. Our starplace. Our starplace.

Eleven girls stayed after school for tryouts the next day, including Tricia and Tanya and Carla and Brenda and Jackie, the five girls I was sure would be chosen, besides Celeste. Tricia sang really well, and so did Brenda. Jackie sort of sounded nervous, and she kept coughing in the middle of her song. This girl named Eugenia, who wasn't any better than I was, sang in this cutesy little girl way that sounded really lame.

Then Miss Cantwell called on Celeste.

Tanya and Carla and Tricia were sitting together in three chairs on the front row. I saw Celeste's eyes flicker nervously toward them while Miss Cantwell played the opening chords.

In the middle of Celeste's first line, Tanya clattered her notebook onto the floor, then Tricia tilted and crashed her chair. Everyone laughed.

Celeste started over and got two lines into her song before Carla had a coughing fit. Tricia scraped her chair legs along the floor, reaching across to pound Carla's back. Other girls in the room started whispering, and a few giggled.

Miss Cantwell stopped playing and looked over her shoulder. "Girls . . ." she warned, but everybody acted innocent, of course.

Celeste started over for a third time. Tricia and Tanya fanned themselves with their math book covers—*whap, whap, whap, whap, whap.*

Celeste quit singing and looked close to tears.

I jumped to my feet. "Dragonbee! There's a deadly dragonbee on Tanya's back!"

Everyone screamed, including Miss Cantwell, and Tanya jumped to her feet and started whirling around, squealing in this little high voice and trying to see her own shoulder blades. I ran down and saved the day by hitting her in the middle of the back with my purse, then quickly wiping the dragonbee residue off and hurrying to bury it deep in the trash can.

"Someone should take her to the restroom to be sure it hasn't *permeated,*" I urgently suggested. I'd just read that lethal-sounding word in a laundry detergent ad the week before.

"I want Tricia to come," Tanya whimpered as she hustled toward the door.

"I don't see anything back there . . ." Tricia said suspiciously as she followed Tanya out.

I flopped down in one of their empty chairs, and while Miss Cantwell played Celeste's opening notes again, I crossed the fingers of one hand and with my other hand touched the bobby pin in my hair. I looked down at the music book in my lap instead of up at Celeste, because if I'd met her eyes I might have giggled and got *her* started giggling.

She was wonderful. She was always wonderful, when people gave her the slightest chance to be.

Miss Cantwell called on me next, and I sang better than I probably ever had. I think it was because I was still so angry at those three girls, and so shocked at myself, and that anger and shock came out in my voice as what Celeste had called "passion."

When Miss Cantwell posted the names of the double trio the next day, Celeste and Tricia were first soprano, Carla and Tanya were second soprano, and Brenda and

Jackie were alto. Miss Cantwell also chose a soprano alternate and an alto alternate, and *I was soprano alternate!* I just couldn't believe it! Me, Frannie Driscoll, soprano alternate for what Miss Cantwell herself had described as potentially the best female choral ensemble in the history of Quiver Junior High!

Two weeks later the girls' double trio had already sung at the First Baptist Church and at Quiver's annual fall festival. They had been asked for not one, but *two* encores at both places. Then Carla went with some friends of her family's to Perch Lake and they ended up waterskiing, though the water temperature was only fifty-some degrees. Carla got a sore throat, which turned into tonsillitis, and she switched from chorus to home economics because she wasn't supposed to strain her throat for at least the rest of the semester.

And that's when I became a full-fledged second soprano in the Ladies of Harmony, which is what the double trio had voted to call themselves.

Ladies of Harmony. When I think of that title and then think of how things worked out that semester, I don't know whether to laugh or cry.

CHAPTER 17

The Ladies of Harmony practiced or performed somewhere at least three evenings a week. By the end of September, the whole town of Quiver seemed to know about us. Most people had heard us sing at a club meeting, or church service, or performing the National Anthem before one of the high school football games. I liked it when some lady would recognize me on the street and I'd hear her whisper to her friend that I was "one of those wonderful young singers."

It's hard to describe how Tricia and Tanya treated Celeste and me now that we were all a part of a winning team, so to speak. They were basically as friendly to us as they were to Jackie and Brenda, the two altos. By that I mean they didn't wave to any of us in the hall or anything, but when we were together practicing with Miss Cantwell, they sometimes said something a little bit nice. Once, for instance, Tanya told Celeste that she liked her new turquoise sweater. If they said obnoxious things about Celeste, or about Celeste and me, I never did hear those things because they at least did it behind our backs, not openly in the restroom like they had those two times before.

Meanwhile, fall suddenly arrived, trailing behind it the most amazing, most beautiful string of weeks ever. Everybody sat in class each day staring out the windows at the gaudy, blazing trees, trying to stay alert enough to say something vaguely relevant if one of the teachers called on us. We lived our *real* lives in the late afternoons, out in the mysterious, sparkling air that held the light till well after eight o'clock each night.

The weather was so irresistible that we actually dug out our old bicycles, though the spring before we'd unanimously decided they looked stupid and we didn't need to go anyplace farther than we could walk. My bike was a black skinny-tired twenty-six inch. Nancy had one a lot like it, only a silly shade of hot pink. Margot had a lumpy green bike with a huge white basket which she told us looked Country French. Kelly had Nibbles.

Celeste's dad let her buy any bike she wanted, so we helped her pick a deep red Schwinn that was classy and perfect for her. She'd never had a bike in St. Louis, but it only took about five minutes to teach her to ride. She used the same system that she used to become one of those song heroines, or the calm Egyptian princess that could negotiate Quiver's hostile blue hallways as gracefully as Cleopatra sailing down the Nile.

She imagined herself riding, then just rode.

The five of us rode out to Jasper Hole nearly every afternoon that Celeste and I weren't singing somewhere. Jasper Hole was basically a deep, wide pit of clear, green water, the biggest of several craters left all along the edges of Minetown when the gravel and zinc had been scooped from the ground. The chat pile mountains rose on all sides, so we could easily imagine it was a lake lost in the middle of the Himalayas, or at least the lower foothills of the Rockies.

It was too cold to swim, but we waded a little. Mostly we picnicked and sprawled on blankets to gossip and giggle. Sometimes we watched Kelly as she galloped around the edge of the Hole, or practiced her roping. Theodore C. Rockman and Max and Jason might trail out with us in the go-cart, then Celeste and Theodore would probably play chess. She'd told the truth that night of the luau—she really wasn't very good. But Theodore mentioned from time to time that she had potential, and I knew he was pretty desperate for a new opponent, since Max was basically the only other person who would still play with him.

I think the fact that Celeste liked the boys made

the rest of us realize we could keep liking them too, even though we were now eighth graders. Even if they drove that go-cart all through high school, Celeste's attitude made us see you can't drop someone you'd miss as much as we would have missed Max, Jason and Theodore.

A few times we stayed at Jasper Hole till it got dusky, then gathered up a little of the old, rotting mineshaft wood that was lying around and had real cookouts. We told ghost stories around the fire, our shadows tall, flickering gremlins against the shining mountains of gravel at our backs.

Funny, but the stories we told were never about the Quiver Serpent, or those miners who'd been buried alive almost directly under where we were sitting. Maybe those stories would have been *too* scary for that place.

One day right at the beginning of October, Miss Cantwell received an invitation on thick Chamber of Commerce letterhead asking the Ladies of Harmony to perform at the annual Chamber Banquet on October 10.

"This is a *hugely* prestigious event," she explained breathlessly. "Years ago some of the high school ensembles were occasionally invited to perform at the Chamber Banquet, but that was before the fund-gobbling football program expanded and the high school music program—I might as well say it, but please don't quote me—crashed and burned. And no one from Quiver *Junior* has ever been invited."

As we left the music room, we caught Miss Cantwell happily slipping the invitation into a little frame in her office she must have rushed out and bought for just that purpose.

"And the banquet's at the Country Club!" I raved to the others at Jasper Hole that evening. "Can you imagine, Celeste and me singing at the *Country Club?* Where they have linen napkins, and fresh flowers on the tables, and you can get caviar and margaritas? The *Country* Club!"

"Oooooo! Mercy me, I do believe I'll faint!" Max teased in a southern-belle voice, shoving his toes deeper into the gravel at the edge of the water.

"*You* can't get margaritas," Nancy corrected.

"The irony is exquisite," Theodore observed. He looked meaningfully across the chessboard at Celeste, she looked back, and they both smiled with their mouths but not their eyes.

"What?" I whined. "You guys! What, what?"

"The Country Club is obviously restricted, Frannie," Celeste said quietly. "It's in Foxgrape Woods to begin with, and almost all country clubs are restricted. I'll probably be the first colored person to be there for anything except to scrub toilets or wash dishes."

"Oh," I said.

*   *   *

I put my dad's dessert plate in front of him a little too hard that night. "If people are good enough to perform complicated musical numbers with three-part harmony, they should be good enough to join the nice place they're nice enough to be performing in, such as a country club. Regardless of what race or creed they happen to be. That's my considered opinion, not the opinion of a mere child."

"Have we got any ice cream for this pie?" Dad asked.

Usually Mom would have been the one to check on that, but she was in the bedroom frantically studying. The realtor's test was in just one week. I went to the freezer and got the ice cream, then opened it and began scraping the layer of frost off.

My hands were shaking a little as I walked over and thunked a double spoonful of runny ice cream on his pie, then went back to the sink to start the dishes.

Pretty soon he said, "Frannie, in a free market society the businessmen who succeed deserve a certain exalted status within the community. When you're older you'll understand that perks such as country club membership are one of the ways democracy encourages and nurtures leadership."

White leadership! I wanted to scream. *Flesh-crayon-colored, Ken-doll-looking, white, white, white!*

I dropped the glass I was scrubbing back into the

137

soapy water and had to pick it up again. Tears were blurring my eyes.

I was afraid they were tears of anger, and that really scared me.

Suddenly, I didn't know if I was being unpatriotic or not. And if I wasn't being unpatriotic, then I was at least being disloyal by doubting my dad's heartfelt beliefs and actually feeling angry with him, which might even be breaking one of the Ten Commandments, the one about honoring your parents.

That night was the last straw. I was sick of being confused about democracy and patriotism and that stuff. I decided I needed to make a huge effort to learn more about current events, so I started watching the six o'clock news on TV. It didn't take long for me to learn who Dr. Martin Luther King was and that he was *not* Celeste's family physician. Some nights the news showed people in the deep South, both black and white, marching to protest the unequal treatment of Negroes. Sometimes they'd be getting onto busses, trying, the news said, to integrate the interstate transportation system. Then you'd see other people, all white, trying to block the people from marching, or from getting on the busses. No matter how peaceful and ordinary-looking everything started out, before long the news cameras were panning over police lines holding back people so angry their faces seemed subhuman. Sometimes you'd see people, black and white, being clubbed by police or dragged off to jail.

The Berlin Wall was in the news, too—*big* time. Next to the local stories about University of Oklahoma football games, it was what you heard about the most. It sounded like if the Wall wasn't torn down, we might have a nuclear war with the Soviet Union at any minute. In fact, we started having almost daily bomb drills at school, getting under our desks while a scary siren screeched and we imagined ourselves being vaporized.

Two nights in a row, the news showed pictures of this jungle, and the newsguys talked like we might be going to have a war in this place called Vietnam. The next night, though, these smart-looking guys in suits called "military advisers" came on and said it wasn't going to happen, so I quit worrying about it and went back to just worrying about the Berlin Wall and those awful, hateful riots.

I also decided to try to read *Time* in my library study halls. That was easier said than done, though, because I got sleepy in there and the *Seventeen*'s were basically the only magazines that could keep me awake.

I was sleepy because Celeste and I had fallen into a pattern of meeting three or four times a week up on the rocket platform, and sometimes we stayed up there really late talking. Sometimes it was so late when we quit that

I'd taken to sneaking back in through my bedroom window, and I think Celeste had, too.

"I love my dad," I told her one night. "He's so smart. He can fix anything."

"I know," she agreed. "He's really neat."

The day before, my dad had fixed a huge nail puncture in Celeste's bike tire. Even though he looked exhausted when he got out of our Plymouth each afternoon, he always came around to the patio before he even went into the house to see if my friends and I were out there and to ask if we needed anything.

"I love my dad too," Celeste said. "He's not that great at fixing things, but he's really smart in all kinds of other ways."

"Boy, I know," I agreed, shaking my head with wonder at Mr. Chisholm.

When we biked past Celeste's house, or stopped in front of it to wait for her to come out on our way to Jasper Hole, you could see her dad through their front screen door, sitting bent over his desk, working away. Or sometimes he'd be on the porch swing, with books spread all around him, writing in a notebook. When he saw us, he'd always stop what he was doing, take off his glasses, smile, and walk over to talk to us. He'd ask us how our day had gone, then listen closely, as though locker jams and algebra mindtangles were the most fascinating things in the world.

"Do you think our dads would like each other? I mean, my dad is a factory foreman and your dad is a professor and everything, but since they're both so smart they might really hit it off, don't you think?"

We were dangling our legs through the vertical bars, and Celeste had her arms folded along the horizontal bar that ran at our chest level. I expected her to answer with a simple "sure" or "yes."

"Maybe," she said. She began bouncing her chin on her hands. "Frannie, when my dad's about done with the research part of his book, then I can talk about it more. But he wouldn't care if I told you this much now. He started it because he wanted to learn as much as he could about my great-grandfather, his grandfather. My Great-grandfather Chisholm was a miner here, way back before the 1920's."

I was totally surprised. For some reason, maybe because of their elegant clothes and manners, I'd assumed Celeste's family had lived in St. Louis for a million years.

"He was killed when he was just thirty-two years old."

I gasped. "Oh, no. He was one of the eleven miners caught in the big cave-in?"

She shook her head no. "Dad's having trouble finding out the details of how he died." She put her cheek in her hand and leaned closer to me. "You know that big sign we pass on Route 66 when we ride along the highway coming back from Jasper Hole?"

"The one the Chamber of Commerce put up?" I snorted. "You mean that big old hokey sign that says, 'Howdy, y'all! Welcome to Quiver, Oklahoma! If you can't stop and shop, at least wave hi as you drive by!' "

You almost *had* to laugh at that sign, but Celeste wasn't laughing. She was grim.

"That's the one. It's supposed to mark the city limits, but strictly speaking, it sits between Minetown and Quiver, and Minetown *is* in the city limits. Back in my great-grandfather's day there used to be a different sign on the same two big wooden poles. Know what *that* sign at the edge of 'white' Quiver said?"

I swallowed. Her tone made me brace myself. "No," I whispered.

"It said, 'Black man, don't dare let the sun set on you here.' "

I put my forehead down on the metal bar and closed my eyes.

"I hope our dads would get along, Frannie," Celeste whispered after a while. "There's so much around here that works against that, though. You know lots of kids still snub me at school, or even say something obnoxious they hope I'll overhear."

She was crying. It was too dark to see tears, but I could just feel it. I edged closer and put an arm around her shoulders.

Pretty soon she straightened her back and wiped her

eyes with her palms. "You know what? My dad went to the college library in Tulsa tonight and he said he wouldn't be home till after I was in bed. I think this is the perfect night for you to finally get the grand tour of my haunted house."

CHAPTER 18

As we walked the seven blocks to Celeste's house that still October night, I tried to calm the twitchy feeling along my neck and spine by reminding myself of how different the house was now that mean Mr. Teschler wasn't sitting on his porch scowling at all the kids who went by. Mr. Chisholm had given it a coat of fresh, shiny white paint, and put up a neat picket fence. Celeste had brought us in as far as the living room several times, and nothing had seemed creepy at all. In fact, it was beautiful, with its newly polished hardwood floors and built-in bookshelves and a shiny black piano in one corner.

"Uh, Celeste? I think you should take those garbage bags off the attic windows," I told her as we walked, mostly to hear the sound of my own voice in the too-quiet darkness. "I mean, no offense, but that's probably why the house still feels haunted to you. My dad says Mr. Teschler blacked out those windows because he used to have creepy parties up there, but he's been dead for two years now and still those awful black . . . *eye*sockets are up there watching everybody who comes down your sidewalk."

We'd reached the corner and turned onto her block. The picket fence was glowing in the luminous darkness ahead of us like a row of even but snaggled teeth.

"No, Frannie, you've got it backwards," Celeste told me, reaching her gate and pushing it open. "We deliberately left those windows covered because the attic's the part of the house that's haunted."

She stood holding the gate open for me. Gulping, I forced myself to walk through, and the gate closed so fast behind us it made me wonder if Mr. Teschler's peeved ghost had kicked it shut.

We went through Celeste's beautiful living room and down a hallway. The hallway was pretty, well-lit and newly painted, but near the end of it a rough opening had been cut in the wall, exposing a set of narrow stairs that led steeply upward to the left.

"This wall was smooth when we moved here," Celeste told me. "There was no way to get up to the attic. Mr. Joslen said the attic opening had probably been just a hole in the ceiling when the house was built, and it had

145

probably gotten closed up during some remodeling project. Dad found this stairway by tapping on the walls."

"But why was he *looking* for a stairway?"

Celeste didn't answer. Instead she took a key from a tiny nail hidden beneath the banister and started up the stairs. As I watched her ankles dissolve in shadows, I found myself mentally repeating the phrase I'd used in this same house last Hallowe'en— *This isn't real, this isn't real, this isn't real!* Somehow, it worked better when you were looking at rubber vampire bats and black-lighted monster masks than it did when you were facing a genuine locked door at the top of a rickety hidden stairway.

"Maybe we should wait until we ask your dad about this," I called up to her.

Celeste turned the key in the lock of the door at the top of the stairway. "Come *on*, Frannie," she said quickly over her shoulder, then shoved open the door and disappeared through it as cleanly as if she'd gone into another dimension.

"Celeste?" Cold fingers riffled along my scalp as I ran to the top of the stairs and followed her over the threshold.

Celeste flicked a switch somewhere and we were suddenly bathed in dim, blueish light.

I'd expected the attic to be one large, cobwebby open area, but that wasn't what it was like up there at all. Celeste and I were facing an unpainted wooden wall that must have been about eight feet high and that ran the whole length of the attic. A narrow walkway had been left along the edge of it, which is where we were standing.

"It's a room," Celeste whispered. "Picture some giant taking the roof off the house, putting a huge shoebox inside that fit almost exactly on the attic floor, then putting the roof back on again to hide it."

"Why would anyone build a room inside a room? I mean, what's it for?"

"Come on," she whispered, leading me down the walkway. "See if you can find the hidden entrance."

I trailed one hand along the wood as we went slowly around the giant's weird shoebox. On the third side, I thought I felt a slot.

"This is so weird," I whispered, crouching to trace the slot to the ground, then stretching to trace it as far over my head as I could reach. "This must be an opening, but where's the doorknob?"

Celeste took the rhinestone bobby pin out of her hair and slipped it into the slot, then wedged it so that the hidden door swung open a few inches.

I don't know if it was the stale air that came rushing from that sealed room, or if it was because I was sandwiched between the wall and the sloping attic rafters in a tight, enclosed space. But suddenly, it seemed to me like the stairway down was too far away for us to ever see again, and I sank to my knees, panting. "Cuh . . . Celeste!"

She dropped beside me and grabbed my shoulders. "It's okay, it's okay."

She waited till I shivered off the worst of my panic, then she asked, "Do you want to go back down, or do you want to look inside?"

With all my heart, I wanted to go back down. "Inside," I croaked.

Celeste smiled and stood, then gave the door a solid heave with her shoulder. It creaked wider open.

Liquid darkness lunged out at us. "There are candles and matches just inside," Celeste whispered as she moved into the awful room and let that darkness swallow her. I held my breath, listening to the blood thump against my eardrums, and a few seconds later I heard the scrape of a match and Celeste was standing holding a fat candle in a circle of light just a few feet away. Near her was a table with more candles and some papers in a heap.

"Come on in," she said.

When I took a small step toward her and let go of the door I'd been gripping, it banged shut behind me so fast I had to hustle out of the way. This wasn't Mr. Teschler's ghost, though—I'd felt some kind of spring. The hidden door had been designed to let you enter quickly, very quickly, before it concealed itself again.

"Here." Celeste lit a candle and held it toward me.

I took it and looked around the room. Old-fashioned wooden lockers lined two walls. That almost made me laugh—a ghostly locker room where spooks stored their damp towels and stinky sneakers?

"It's so . . . tiny in here. It looks so much bigger from the outside."

"This is just a sort of antechamber. The giant's shoe-box is divided into two tiny rooms like this and a main room that's much larger. Come on."

She led me into the other small room. No lockers. Just a big table that looked like it had been carefully set in the exact middle of the room. It had some kind of fancy, shiny tablecloth with an elaborate moon and star design on it that gave me the creeps.

"Thanks for showing me this stuff, Celeste," I whispered, "but I guess we better get back down now before . . ."

"You haven't seen the big room, yet," Celeste said. Her voice was totally flat, without any of its usual musical lilt. She held her candle higher and turned as though in a trance to solemnly lead the way back through the other small room and then through another doorway cut between the rows of lockers.

The big room, at first, seemed totally empty, then I noticed a bunch of old-fashioned metal folding chairs thrown into one corner like broken toys. Several other

149

chairs had been covered with the same shiny material as the tablecloth in the small room, and they were arranged facing the center of the room in some kind of weird kaleidoscopic design.

Celeste walked to the far left corner of the room. When she got close, her candle illuminated a sort of little raised platform there, with a desk and chair set up on it. The desk was covered with a creepy tablecloth matching the one in the small room.

I guess I didn't realize how totally silent it was until suddenly a scurrying, scratching sound started up right over our heads. My heart slammed and I felt a big pulse of blood travel instantly from my toes to hit my brain.

"Celeste!" I hissed, dizzy with fright.

To my horror, I saw fear in her eyes, too. "Let's go," she said quickly.

As she hurried back, her candle gave me a clear look at something in the very center of the room. It was one of those things preachers stand behind when they talk. No. It was wider and flatter. Wider than a pulpit, taller than a table. It had dark stains on it.

We were practically running when we went back through the little room with the lockers. Our breeze caused one of the lockers to gape open. A flicker of ghostly white reached out to us from the gloom inside.

The hinge on that hidden door slammed it tight the second we'd escaped back through, thank goodness.

★   ★   ★

"Well, what did you think?"

I closed my eyes and tried to let the porch swing rock that scurrying sound and that flash of glowing white right out of my head.

"You must have an opinion," Celeste pressed.

I licked my dry lips. "Do *you* know what it's for? Satanic rights? Devil worship? That thing in the center of the big room is . . . is an altar, right?"

Celeste nodded solemnly. "I know what the room is for, but my dad won't let me talk about it yet." She stopped the swing with her heels to make me open my eyes and look at her. "But Frannie, I'll tell you this much. You're more right than wrong."

Mr. Chisholm drove up a few minutes later, and when he offered me a ride home I jumped at it.

No way could I have willingly walked all those dark blocks by myself that night.

CHAPTER 19

When Mr. Chisholm let me out in our driveway, I thought I'd be in trouble for getting home late, especially since all the downstairs lights were on. Normally after ten o'clock the only light you could have seen through our living room picture window would have been the fuzzy flicker of the evening news on TV.

Then I noticed that the house *sounded* funny, too. Rock and roll? The new Chubby Checker dance record Margot had loaned me, blasting from our living room stereo when *I* wasn't even *home?* "Let's do the twist!" Chubby Checker urged at the top of his lungs.

Then two exact replicas of my mother and my father jerked past the picture window, gyrating their hips, swiveling out their elbows, throwing around their usually carefully plastered-down hair and laughing, laughing, laughing.

"Round and round and up and down!" Chubby Checker sang. My father grabbed a plastic rose from the vase on the TV and clenched it between his teeth.

I'd thought Celeste's attic was awful, but this was *really* scary. The only possible explanation was that I was caught in the middle of *The Twilight Zone* from two weeks ago, the one about plantlike aliens that took over human bodies.

The father replica spotted me. He flung open the front door, still twisting. My stomach knotted in revulsion, and I glanced over my shoulder to see if any of the neighbors were watching.

"Frannie!" he—*it,* the father mutant—called out to me. "We're celebrating! Your mother aced her realtor's test today! She scored so high they had to check the results *three times* before they could believe them!"

After that strange night's many "twists" and turns, I couldn't get to sleep. I lay staring out my window at the spot in the alley where Jay used to park, but didn't any longer because he'd joined the Navy last month, people said to avoid marrying Charlotte. I stared through the field which, in spite of the warm weather, was becoming autumn-brittle and spiderweb-coated. I focused on the rocket that six weeks ago had seemed like only a rusty splinter, but that had become our starplace, Celeste's and mine. Then I shifted my focus to the lights crawling tirelessly along Route 66. Did the people in those Fords and Chevys and Oldsmobiles believe in their hearts that when they got to wherever they were going their lives would be uncomplicated?

I had the sudden urge to talk to Robin.

It shocked me to realize I hadn't talked to him at all since the luau five weeks ago. No one had snuck into my brain to talk to me, either. Not the Olympic skating announcer, not Dick Clark, not the narrator of the detective story I starred in, not the art curator who'd loved my papier mâché sculpting so much. None of them.

I sighed. "Oh, Robin, my love, my . . ."

This was stupid. He was just a cartoon, and even if he'd been real he would have had about a dozen perfectly gorgeous Hollywood girlfriends.

I flopped onto my stomach, pulled the pillow over my head and went to sleep.

Two nights later, the Ladies of Harmony performed at the Chamber of Commerce Banquet at Foxgrape Country Club. It went without a hitch. We even got to eat before it, at a table with a white tablecloth and fresh flowers.

"We have lunch in this room after we swim in the summer," Tricia informed the other five of us at the table, looking only at Tanya.

"You don't even have to wear shoes or real clothes,"

Tanya added, looking only at Tricia. "Just a beach jacket over your suit, and flip flops on your feet. The swimming pool's on the other side of that wall of drapes over there. In summer they open these big sliding glass doors that are behind those drapes, and whenever you're hungry . . ."

". . . or thirsty," Tricia added.

"Yeah, or thirsty, you just get out of the water and—presto!—you're in here eating."

Celeste, Brenda, Jackie and I just sat there, thinking about it. To this day, when I imagine true luxury, I picture myself coming up dripping out of a pool, sticking my feet into rubber flip flops, and walking thirty feet to get fed anything I want at a table with a white cloth and flowers.

After we sang, and even after we'd used up our two encore numbers, the applause took a long time to die down. Miss Cantwell was glowing, partly with perspiration but surely partly with happiness.

She gave a little concluding speech to the audience while we still stood in our performance semi-circle behind her, smiling our faces off.

"These girls have exceeded all my expectations this fall, and my newest dream is to take them to the regional showchoir competition in Tulsa this winter. This is a very selective invitational event, but I'm pleased to announce that on the basis of a tape I recently sent to the officials in Tulsa, our Ladies of Harmony have been pre-qualified!"

There was loud whooping and applause while we six stood frozen as popsicles in our best Sunday pastel dresses, trying to figure out what all this meant.

"Our only slight obstacle will be the three-hundred-dollar registration fee, which I'll be discussing with the school administrators on Monday," Miss Cantwell concluded when the applause had died to whispering and smiling around the room.

A man jumped to his feet. Tricia's eyes widened and she stiffened, so I figured he was her father, and she was terrified that he was about to do something embarrassing.

"As the Chamber's finance chairman, I move we *pay* that fee to show our pride and support for these beautiful young ladies!" he boomed, and about three seconds later there was unanimous agreement.

Miss Cantwell glowed even brighter, and she hadn't just finished working hard directing us this time, so I knew it was one-hundred percent from happiness, not sweat.

Five days later, though, Miss Cantwell's bubble suddenly burst.

"Dresses," she uttered bleakly as the six of us lined up for an after-school practice that day.

She was sitting at the piano, and she let the glossy catalog she'd been looking through slide from her fingers onto the piano bench. It riffled itself off the end and onto the floor as Miss Cantwell slumped forward and let her elbow hit three jarring notes on the keyboard.

Jackie picked the catalog up from the floor, and the other five of us gathered quickly to look at it over her shoulder.

"That's a brochure about formal performance dresses I received with the registration forms from Tulsa today," Miss Cantwell explained without turning around. "It says in the material they sent that besides being judged for musicality, we'll be judged on 'style and conformity of attire,' and they included that catalog to illustrate what's expected."

"Ohmygosh," Jackie breathed. "Some of these dresses cost three-hundred dollars!"

"For six?" I asked, which must not have seemed like a very stupid question, because even Tricia waited for Miss Cantwell to answer.

"For just one," Miss Cantwell said in a squeezed voice. "Some are as much as five-hundred dollars, and none are less than one-hundred-and-fifty dollars. The school doesn't have anywhere near that kind of money to budget for such a thing. And we can't ask your parents to spend that kind of money on one satin dress."

No one said a word. There were two, possibly three,

girls in the group whose parents could have afforded one of those dresses. Tricia and Celeste for sure, Tanya probably. I was kind of surprised that Tricia didn't speak up and say her parents would be glad to buy her one.

"Let's skip rehearsal for just today, girls," Miss Cantwell whispered. She got up and hurried into her office. She was probably crying, though I was relieved to not hear or see anything to make me sure of that. It was strange enough to run across a teacher out of her usual classroom setting, like in the grocery store or somewhere. I couldn't even imagine seeing one doing something like crying.

CHAPTER 20

A couple of days after Miss Cantwell's big dreams slammed into that brick wall, all the eighth grade physical education classes went bowling together at Quiver's state-of-the-art, twenty-four lane Lucky Strike Bowl-A-Rama.

"I don't see what bowling has to do with physical education," Nancy grumbled while we stood in the crunch of people yelling out sizes to the three overworked clerks who were checking out bowling shoes.

"It isn't exercise for you, Nancy, because you just walk up to the fault line and drop your ball," Kelly explained. "People who really lunge with their legs and swing the ball from the shoulder and take running steps for momentum get exercise."

"Oh!" Nancy said, like that had never occurred to her.

"I don't believe I shall indulge in this sport today," Theodore C. Rothman informed us as he began strolling over to the row of orange plastic chairs by the fudgesicle machine.

Mr. Tenant, our gym teacher, saw Theodore leave the crowd but didn't make him come back. He'd probably been briefed by our seventh grade gym teacher about last year, when one of Theodore's balls had jumped his lane and landed on the toe of a luckily nice lady, who had smiled sweetly even as she limped out to her car.

In my opinion, bowling was kind of fun. The sweaty checking-out-shoes crunch was the only bad part. Kelly and Celeste and I worked our way to the front of the shoe check-out mob at just about the same time.

"Size seven," I called out.

"Eight-and-a-half," Kelly called out.

"Seven," I heard Celeste mumble.

Two of the clerks turned quickly to the shoe rack behind them, then slammed pairs of black and white shoes in front of Kelly and me. "Next!" they ordered.

The clerk in front of Celeste murmured, "Excuse me a second," and left.

She came back a minute later with the greasy-haired man who owned the lanes. His name was tattooed on his arm below the roll of Camels in his t-shirt sleeve—RUFUS.

Rufus dug in his ear with his little finger and glared

at Celeste as he jerked the thumb on his other hand toward a sign posted on the wall behind him: WE RESERVE THE RIGHT TO REFUSE SERVICE TO ANYONE.

"Store policy," he explained in a flat voice.

Celeste's eyes were bright with embarrassment. I could feel her straining to escape back through the crowd, so I grabbed her by the sleeve to make her stay.

"We're here with our school!" I bleated.

"Store policy," Rufus repeated, sounding bored. "I'll let her bowl all right, but she can't rent shoes, for sanitary reasons."

He took a grayish toothpick from his shirt pocket and stuck it in his mouth, then ducked under the counter and went back to wherever he'd been before.

The clerk's neck was bright pink. She licked her lips. "Next," she said, desperately trying to pretend Celeste wasn't there.

I looked frantically around for Mr. Tenant, and was relieved to see *he'd* seen what was happening and had waylaid Rufus over in the corner by the pin-ball machines. I saw them talking animatedly, though Mr. Tenant seemed to be doing more pleading than demanding.

Rufus came fuming back to the check-in counter, bent to rummage through some kind of box he kept on the floor, and slammed a pair of gawdy green and black bowling shoes in front of Celeste. He sucked hard and loudly on his toothpick and didn't look at her.

"Leave them shoes over by the ball stands when you're through. I'll be wanting to spray them before I put them back up."

I picked up the shoes and pulled Celeste backwards till we were finally out of the crowd.

"Did you guys *see* that?" I asked Nancy and the others, and they nodded, looking as numb and helpless as I felt.

"Who does he think he is?" Max huffed, his hands on his hips.

"The owner," Celeste answered in a small voice. "Haven't you guys ever noticed a sign like that before? They've got them up in restaurants all over the place. Every time I see one I know what's coming, and I just want to . . . hide."

"I've *seen* those signs, but I thought they meant if someone starts a fight or something they can get kicked out," Margot said, which is what I'd thought, too.

Theodore appeared, like he always did when there was a concept to explain.

"More often those signs are used, as Celeste has pointed out, as a not-very-subtle statement of the owner's bigotry," he told us. "In a privately owned establishment, integration can't be legislated as easily as it can in a public facility, such as a school."

"I'm sorry," Jason said sadly, touching Celeste's wrist.

Theodore planted one finger on the tape holding his

glasses together. "Do you remember the stories on the news a year or so ago about the Woolworth's sit-ins? A waitress refused to serve some black students at a lunch counter over in North Carolina, and they just kept sitting there until they were arrested. But the arrests triggered protests, and every day more people showed up to join the sit-in at that counter, until finally people were crowding around everywhere and business was seriously disrupted in that part of town. Economics came into play where the law couldn't, and—wallah! To end the impasse, nearby lunch counters were finally desegregated."

"This isn't a social studies quiz, Theodore!" I snapped, shaking all over. "She's supposed . . . she's actually supposed to leave her shoes over by the ball stand so that awful Rufus can *spray* them with some kind of disinfectant or something after she wears them!"

"I shall be requiring your shoes, Max," Theodore said, and held out one rigid index finger.

Max draped his bowling shoes over Theodore's finger by the looped laces, and Theodore walked over to the ball stands, sat down cross-legged on the floor, and tossed the shoes onto the carpet a few feet in front of him.

"Let's *all* leave our shoes to be sprayed," he suggested.

The eight of us quickly formed a circle on the floor and tumbled our bowling shoes into a pile in the middle. Pretty soon, some other kids quit bowling and joined us. By the time Mr. Tenant told us to load the busses that day, there were at least thirty of us surrounding a pile of sixty-some bowling shoes, all but two of them identical black and white.

It was going to be hard to match that heap of look-alike shoes into pairs. Rufus was fuming when we left, and Mr. Tenant was flustered. The college kids behind the check-in counter were smiling, though, and one of them snuck Celeste a thumbs-up sign.

I don't imagine our tiny sit-in had much effect on the economic future of the Bowl-A-Rama, but I *do* think it made Celeste feel a little better. Especially the fact that those other kids had joined us. Who knows how much her simple presence at Quiver Junior could eventually have changed things?

If it just hadn't been for those awful formal dresses.

The story about the dresses was in that night's *Quiver Gazette,* even before two-thirds of us in the Ladies of Harmony knew what had happened.

"Here's something about your double trio and that performance in Tulsa you told us about," Dad said, tilting the paper toward me. "Thought you said Miss Cantwell had given up the idea of going."

"It was a competition, and she has," I murmured. I was sprawled on the floor near his feet, fiddling with algebra and thinking about the bowling shoes, but I looked up and tilted my head to read the headline:

LOCAL BUSINESS COALITION PLEDGES MONEY TO SUPPORT SCHOOL MUSIC COMPETITION. Beneath it was a picture of Miss Cantwell accepting a check from a group of people, one of whom I recognized as being Tricia's father.

"That must have been written before Miss Cantwell learned how expensive competing was going to be." I sighed and squinted at my book again. "The Chamber of Commerce was going to pay the registration fee, but now they won't have to."

"Says here, 'A group of community-minded businesspeople has pledged up to eighteen-hundred dollars to purchase competition-quality performance gowns for . . .' "

I bounced to my knees and snatched the paper, then began skimming for details. ". . . in addition to this generous money gift, a committee of mothers has been formed to help in the selection of the dresses . . . has been explained by the donors to be a fundamental investment in the talents of our . . . Miss Cantwell, junior high music instructor, has declared this gift unprecedented and breathtaking in its generosity . . ."

I let the paper fall to the floor and sat back on my heels, my head spinning.

It was hard to get firm details at school the next day, because Miss Cantwell was practically incoherent with joy. Was there some other little thing in her actions, too—some little shadow of confusion or dread—or am I remembering that wrong?

"Basically," she told us breathlessly at afterschool practice, "when Tricia and Tanya told their parents about the dresses being so expensive, their mothers and some friends had a long discussion and finally agreed that yes, it was a lot of money, but on the other hand you can't put a price on this kind of opportunity!"

She bounced on her heels a couple of times while Tricia and Tanya basked in their new heroine status. The rest of our rehearsal we chattered happily about which dresses to order. All of us understood that the "mothers committee" would do the actual choosing and would undoubtedly pick the high-neck turquoise, but we girls unanimously picked the low-cut gold lamé anyway.

"There's one other thing," Miss Cantwell mentioned as we were getting ready to leave. "I should tell you that Carla has now fully recovered from the unfortunate throat infection she contracted this fall, and has expressed the wish to rejoin the group."

My breath caught in my throat. I coughed, and that little time-out somehow gave me enough grace and equilibrium to realize it was fair that she come back, and that I, after all, was only her alternate. It was fair. I could deal with it. I could.

"That's okay," I managed to say, and shrugged as

nonchalantly as I could, hoping I wouldn't start crying until I was home, or at least in one of the restroom stalls. I mostly hoped I wouldn't accidentally turn and catch Celeste's eye. *Don't worry about me,* I willed her. *I can handle it, but don't look at me right now, okay?*

"Uh, Frannie, I've given it some thought and decided that instead of automatically replacing you with Carla, we should probably re-audition all seven of you on Monday," Miss Cantwell said. She bent to open the piano bench and began searching for a piece of music. "Blends change, and we want things to be as absolutely balanced as they can be for an event this important and . . . well, expensive."

This was a kind of reprieve, and though I knew I would almost certainly be the one left behind after the new audition, I looked over at Celeste and smiled with relief.

She smiled back, but it was the kind of smile she'd smiled that day at Jasper Hole, when I'd been babbling happily about our group singing at the country club.

Celeste smiled at me with her mouth, but not her eyes.

CHAPTER 21

I buried Janice under one of the juniper bushes the next morning, and when I came into the kitchen after washing my hands my mother was making her special good-luck pancakes, the ones shaped like stars. She started making those back when I was in third grade, the morning I was going to my fourth piano lesson and hoping Mrs. Kaputnik would give me a little foil star sticker to show I'd mastered the first piece in my book. I got my star that day, and five years later we were still having star pancakes for breakfast whenever one of us needed good luck.

"Well, everybody can wish *me* luck this morning!" Mom announced as she finished the first batch. She flipped two onto Harley's plate, and two onto Mitch's.

"Creeping hands to strangle yourself with!" Mitch shrieked, picking up a pancake and dangling it in

Harley's face. They both squirmed all over their chairs, laughing.

I indulged in a quick laugh, too. I'd never noticed it before, but Mom's star pancakes *did* look like hands.

Dad came into the kitchen. He leaned back against the counter and said, "So today's the big day, right, Caroline?"

Mom had her back to us, pouring batter. "Since I'll be the only one in the office this morning besides Mr. Joslen, I think this is the ideal time to talk to him about giving me Bob Morgan's job," she said. I could tell she was nervous, but trying not to sound like it.

Bob Morgan was one of Mr. Joslen's brokers. He was retiring in November, and it had been Mom's big dream through all her months of studying for her license to move into his job when he left.

"Piece of cake, with a score like yours," I told her, and Dad smiled his agreement.

"What are your plans today, Franniebannie?" he asked.

I shrugged. "Margot and Nancy are busy, but Celeste and I are biking out to Kelly's to ride horses and stuff."

Mom handed me a plate of hand-stars, and I hurried to the table with it. If Dad asked "what kind of stuff?" I'd have to slightly fib, which was easier when you were eating. You could always mumble something unintelligible and point to your full mouth.

Last week, out at Jasper Hole, Kelly had mentioned that there were wooded, rocky areas around the mines that you could get to only on horseback, and that there was even a little-known cave just beyond the minefields. Celeste had immediately gotten super-interested, and Kelly had promised to take her riding back there sometime.

"You mean that stretch of wilderness over near the bluffs?" Margot had asked. "C'est cra-*zee!* There are rattlesnakes in those rocks."

"And the ground is honeycombed with old rotten mine tunnels," Nancy added, clucking her tongue. "If you fall through clear to China, don't come crying to us."

"Okay, we won't," Kelly had agreed.

I was hoping Celeste would be discouraged by the thought of those rattlesnakes, but every day since she'd reminded Kelly of her promise. Even fearless Kelly seemed reluctant to follow through, but it was getting more obvious all the time that Celeste wasn't going to let it drop.

So that day Kelly, Celeste and I were riding three of Kelly's horses out to see the cave at the far edge of the minefields, to the wilderness area Kelly called Spooklight Hollow.

To be perfectly honest, horseback riding has never brought out the best in me. Kelly was always telling me to relax, that Heathcliff was so gentle you couldn't fall off if you tried, but every time I got on him I felt like I was constantly listing to the left, and the ground looked a mile away. I grasped him so hard with my knees that my bottom ached as we followed the narrow path along the outer edge of the minefields that day.

Ahead of me, Celeste leaned gracefully forward to rub Amelia's neck, and Amelia tossed her mane and whinnied in an appreciative way.

Kelly glanced back from her place in the lead. "Celeste knows horses, which is why I gave her Amelia," she informed us. "Amelia's pretty highstrung, but fun to ride if you handle her right. Heathcliff is so old and gentle you couldn't fall off him even if you . . ."

"I know, I know, Kelly!" I snapped, feeling myself tilt, tilt, tilt to the left.

The sun was hot but the day was breezy and cool. Celeste and Kelly kept exclaiming over some beautiful blazing oak tree or some white cloud shaped like a pirate ship and drifting like a dream, all of which I would have just *loved* to see if I'd dared lift my eyes from Heathcliff's broad and treacherous shoulders.

"Seems like we've been riding for years," I muttered irritably.

"Let's stop here a minute," Kelly said.

She slid easily off Nibbles. Celeste patted Amelia again, and Amelia sort of lowered her head to let her swing off easily, too. Heathcliff just stood there like he was stuffed, and I remembered my least favorite thing about riding. You have to get off. That was hard enough at Kelly's ranch with ranch hands around to help.

"I think I'll just stay up here," I told them, squirming to ease my sore bottom. I looked around. We'd come along the highway, then through the scrub brush and past the gravel pyramids. We'd skirted Jasper Hole at least half an hour ago, which was the farthest I'd been into the minefields, until now.

Now we were in the middle of a strange, flat plain of packed red dirt. Even in the cheerful sunshine it was eery.

"I've never heard this kind of . . . quiet," Celeste whispered.

"No birds," Kelly said. "No trees for them. Under our feet are the first mines ever dug around here. For some reason, the trees above them died and won't grow back."

Kelly began pointing out some strange metal circles sticking up an inch or so through the red mud. They were only about as big around as a tennis ball can.

"Air shafts," she explained. "Listen."

She picked up a piece of gravel and dropped it through one of the circles. We heard it falling down, down, down with a spooky slow-motion echoing rhythm—*whuh . . . whuh . . . whuh . . . whuh . . . whuh . . . whuh.* It never seemed to hit bottom.

"Those trees ahead there are Spooklight Hollow."
Kelly handed a piece of gravel to Celeste, who dropped
it down a shaft. *Whuh, whuh, whuh.* "Every night you can
see a bright light moving along the road between the
Hollow and where we're standing now. Some nights you
can see it clear from Minetown. Probably it's caused by
gas from these old mines, but the Indians who lived in
the Hollow before the mine owners bought it always
claimed it was the ghost of an ancient Indian warrior.
He'd lost his head in some battle, and so he came out of
Osage Cave each night to search for it with a lantern.
You saw the spooklight and heard that old story when
we had that hayride a couple of years ago, remember
Frannie?"

I nodded, swallowing. I'd had no idea we were quite
so close to the area where that . . . that headless *thing* actually . . . *walked.*

"So that means we're getting near the cave you talked
about," Celeste said eagerly.

I didn't like that eagerness. "Of course, it'd be stupid
to actually go very *near* the actual *opening* of the cave," I
said. "We all agree about that, right?"

But they were both remounting their horses and
didn't answer.

Inside the dense, woodsy tangle of Spooklight Hollow it was slow-going, even for the horses. As brambles

tore at my tennis shoes, for once I was glad Heathcliff was so tall.

"There's the mouth of the cave," Kelly suddenly announced. We'd been riding without talking, letting the horses concentrate on picking their way. Kelly's voice startled the zillions of insects around us into frantic attack mode. The seesaw chant of locusts and the dive-bombing hiss of tiny stinging things got so loud it was deafening. I clamped my hands over my ears and held even tighter with my knees as Heathcliff plodded on.

Ahead, Kelly stopped in front of a mound of tangled goldenrod and wild berries. She jumped down from Nibbles and started kicking at the tangle with her boots. Celeste pulled up, slid from Amelia, and began yanking at the wild grape vines that seemed to enclose the weed and berry mound like scrawny, protective arms. I found a tree stump and managed to gingerly work my way off Heathcliff, and by the time I joined them, they'd uncovered an old broken sign suspended from three strands of rusty barbed wire. Looking closer, I saw that the barbed wire was pulled across a wide, dark hole in a stone hump that had been hidden completely by goldenrod and berry tangle.

Osage Cave, the faded sign read. *No Trespassing.*

A horsefly stung Amelia, and she whinnied and angrily stomped the ground. The bugs swarmed in a thick cloud around us, an airsquad intent on driving the enemy away. I, for one, was more than willing to retreat. My hair felt matted with spiderwebs. I itched all over, even my eyeballs.

"Well, that's that," I said. "No trespassing. It would have been fun to get a look inside, but you guys see the sign, so let's start back. You . . . guys?"

Kelly had taken leather gloves from her saddlebag and was stretching apart the strands of barbed wire, and Celeste was hunching small and sliding through. On the other side of the sign she peered into the dark cave, then took one step and was swallowed by opaque blackness.

"You're next, Frannie. Don't snag your hair on the wire going under," Kelly said.

At first, being inside the cave was a surprising relief. The mouth had been small and claustrophobic, but the walls quickly widened and gained height as the path through the rock sloped sharply downward. The only sunlight came from the entrance, a diminishing oval of light at our backs, but Kelly had produced two butane lanterns from her deep saddlebags. It was cool and bugless, which was sheer bliss after the sweaty, buggy haze of the past hour or so. Nice and quiet, too. The deafening locust chant faded into the distance with every step we took. It reminded me of the way the annoying, staticky music on Jay's car radio used to fade as he snuck from our alley each night.

But then the steep path got steeper and rounded a corner, and the oval of sunshine behind us closed like an eye. The lanterns threw a pale wash of light on things, but didn't really *light* them. The ceiling was black, the walls were swirling purplish shadows. We took turns holding the lanterns, because whoever didn't have one kept stubbing her toes on stones that jabbed up from the floor.

My sweaty clothes stuck to my skin. I started intensely missing all that buggy, sunshiny messiness, all that awful teeming life outside in the light. Would Janice's slimy ghost haunt a place like this?

Suddenly, there was a leathery *whuck-whuck-whuck* right over our heads. I screamed, one little yelp that echoed twice. Kelly swung her light overhead, and we saw a colony of bats hanging upside down, staring at us with pinpoint eyes.

"Cover your hair with your arms!" I screeched. "Bats love hair!"

"Bats are blind," Kelly stated. "How could they see to find hair? Besides, they're not going anywhere. They're trying to sleep. We just temporarily disturbed them."

There was a coppery taste in my mouth. Or was it a smell? You couldn't tell taste from smell in here. Everything was watery air like a salamander would breath.

A panicky gnawing was starting in my stomach just

like the day we'd been up in Celeste's attic. What if we couldn't find our way out of here?

And then Kelly's lantern reflected back something that wasn't darkness. A wall of stone loomed right ahead of us. "Is that . . . where the cave ends?" I called up, hopefully.

"Must be."

"Look at this." Celeste crouched and picked up a fat stick, more of a tree branch that had been lying on the floor. One end was black and crumbly. "This was someone's torch, maybe from back before they had flashlights or even gas lanterns."

There were other branches just like it scattered around. And a circle of stones with some blackened, crumbling logs in the middle. Someone's campfire.

"Whoa," Kelly breathed. "Get a load of this."

She'd been running her lantern across the graffiti which covered the semicircle of stone where the sides of the cave came together to form its back wall. But now she focused her light directly on two chains that were hanging straight down from the stone wall like black, skeletal arms. A C-shape of metal dangled from the bottom of each one like an open claw.

"What . . . *are* those?" I whispered. "Some kind of . . . handcuffs?"

"Manacles," Celeste answered quickly. "You know, like in dungeons. Like in old horror movies, the dungeons in the castles have . . . manacles chained to the walls."

Kelly stood looking at them and shaking her head. "I'll bet when Oklahoma was just a territory marshalls used this cave as an overnight stopping place when they took prisoners somewhere more than a day's ride away."

I walked over and touched the strange black things, then lifted one of them. It was much heavier than it looked, moist with condensation, and very cold. It looked just like one of those bangle bracelets, the kind you tried on at the drugstore. A thick, dull-black bangle bracelet. This size would have been too big for me, probably. There was only one way to find out which ones really fit, and which ones looked right but turned out to be too big. I slipped my wrist inside and squeezed the two edges, and they closed together with a snappy click.

"Frannie!" Celeste screamed. Kelly was looking at my wrist with her eyes sort of bugged out and her mouth open.

A split second too late, I realized this wasn't the drugstore, and I'd just locked myself up.

CHAPTER 22

Kel-*leee!* Get me out! Get me out, Kelly, getmeout-getmeout! KellyKellyKelly!"

I yanked and yanked, trying to squeeze my hand through, but the bracelet didn't turn out to be too big after all.

They both rushed over and Celeste grabbed my arm above the elbow. "Frannie? Calm. Down." She put her other hand on my cheek and turned me so I was looking in her eyes, not down at that awful iron claw. "You hear me, star sister? Calm down before you make yourself sick."

"I can't calm down!" My heart had turned to an engine that was trying to pump itself right out of my chest. I didn't blame it—who wouldn't want out of a body fastened to this awful damp wall? This must be exactly how animals felt right before they chewed off a foot to escape a trap!

I grabbed her shoulder. "Don't leave me!" I whimpered. "Please, please, please don't leave me here!"

She rolled her eyes and leaned back against the wet wall so she was as close to me as she could get. "You know it's ridiculous to even *think* I'd do that."

Kelly had been fiddling with my iron bracelet, but she gave up with a sigh. "It's locked tight. It'll take me about forty-five minutes to gallop to the ranch for help, and maybe twenty for them to load into the Jeep and get back here. We've got a ranch hand that knows black-smithing. He can surely get this off. Surely."

That word "surely" nearly sent me over the edge again, but I bit my lips and nodded.

"Kelly?" Celeste said. "Go to my house too and get my dad and tell him exactly what's happened. Ask if he's ever found a key upstairs that might possibly have been used for manacles like these. He'll want to come back here with you. You won't talk him out of it, so let him."

A lot of that needed a ton of explaining, but Kelly just said, "Right."

"I want . . . I want my dad too," I whimpered.

"Three dads and a blacksmith. Got it," Kelly said, then grabbed the smaller of the two lanterns, turned on her heel, and started running. We listened to the echo of her boots slip-sliding as she hustled along the wet stone path.

"What if . . . what if our light goes out?" I whispered. "Runs out of fuel or something?"

"These go for several hours, and Kelly filled it to the top."

"But anything could happen! A rock slide could start, or one of those rattlesnakes could show up. Or the bats could attack! Anything could happen, Celeste. Anything. And you . . . you couldn't help running away, it would just be human nature to run away if, like, if that beheaded Indian started to appear. Oh, Celeste, you'd automatically have to run away, and I'd be in here . . . in here *alone!*"

Celeste sighed and shook her head at me, then picked up the other chain, put her hand in the empty bracelet, and clicked it closed.

"Satisfied, silly?"

I had never seen anybody do anything more shocking. To this day, I still haven't. I closed my jabbering mouth and just nodded, thunderstruck.

"Now, Frannie," Celeste said, her eyes glistening in the lamplight, "I think the time has come for you to hear the story of my great-grandfather and of the old Teschler house and of the field. It'll take your mind off your hand, and this may be the last real chance I'll have to talk to you about it all, if things . . . well, this may be the only chance I'll get. My dad's sure he has the whole story pieced together now, and I want to tell you everything, all of it. But you've got to tell me first you can listen and not have a part of yourself fearing the dark in here or spooks or what people will think when they come to rescue us or anything else, because this is a tale that needs to be heard wholeheartedly or not at all."

"But Celeste, what do you mean it may be the last—"

"Heard and remembered, Frannie. All right?"

I suddenly realized she was asking me to prove I could do what I'd promised to try to do up in our starplace that first night. Right now was when I was supposed to leave every last bit of wimpy fear behind so I could give her every bit of my heart.

"I promise," I whispered, trying to breathe deeply, in and out, in and out.

She pulled the rhinestone bobby pin from her hair, and I pulled mine from my hair, and with our two free hands we looped them and stood holding them by the open ends. The lantern caught the sparkles and threw them into dancing light-shapes on the rough stone we leaned against, each of us with one arm yanked back at a crazy angle.

"Okay, here goes," Celeste said, then she took a deep breath and lifted her chin. "Okay. My great-grandfather's name was Lewis Chisholm, and my father says he came to Oklahoma from Tennessee in 1903, when he was only fifteen. His parents both died of a flu epidemic that broke out near Memphis at about the turn of the century. They'd had a small farm, but it wouldn't support all five of the kids who were left behind, so one day Lewis just started walking. This is where he was when the soles of his shoes wore through, and he was hired right off at the mines.

"People liked him. He played the harmonica, which he called the mouth organ, and he told jokes."

The *harmonica?* My mind spun, but I didn't dare interrupt.

"I picture him as looking like my dad, only laughing more. I mean, he wasn't a big reader and studier like my dad, which can make you sort of serious about life. I picture my dad's grandfather being not that worried about life, but loving it a lot. Know what I mean?"

I nodded.

"He married my great-grandmother when they were both twenty. Belle, my great-grandmother, had come here from New Orleans when she was nineteen. Belle was a seamstress, and she came here with her aunt, who was a milliner. A milliner makes hats, which there was a big call for back then. My father thinks they left New Orleans because there were tons of good seamstresses and milliners in New Orleans and none here. Belle means 'beautiful' in French. People mostly talked French in New Orleans back then. Every man in Minetown wanted Belle, but Lewis got her."

Celeste stopped for a minute, smiling. It was easy for me to picture beautiful, creative Belle. In my mind's eye, she looked just like her great-granddaughter.

"Belle made fancy dresses for the white ladies in Quiver. All the years she lived, my great-grandmother would go on muleback from Minetown to Quiver and would go into the ladies' houses by the back doors and take their measurements on her knees and then come back to Minetown to whip up what they wanted. In a letter we have she told a friend of hers back in Louisiana that when those ladies gave her a paper pattern to use, she always cut the dress an inch or two bigger than the pattern. If they said they were a twelve she could always figure by eye that they were at least a fourteen or sixteen. She was a very popular seamstress, not only because she was good, but because she played along and made those ladies feel as skinny as they wanted to feel."

I laughed, and that made me realize the panic that had been chewing my insides with sharp teeth was gone, mostly anyway. "Belle sounds . . . what's the word? Shrewd."

"A person of color *had* to be shrewd to survive in places like this. I told you about the sign, Frannie. The one at the edge of town? If you were Negro or dark Indian, you mined for the white men in Quiver, or you sewed and made fancy hats for their wives, but you kept to your place in Minetown after dark, and you kept your head bowed all the time. Knowing how to make a good living like a human and yet act humble as a mule *took* shrewdness, is how I picture it. And daily courage. I think Lewis and Belle both had daily courage, but . . . I guess Lewis didn't have all that much shrewdness. This is where the story turns sad, Frannie, so brace yourself."

But *she* looked like the one who needed bracing. I gave my bobby pin a yank of support, and she looked at me, then took a deep breath and went on.

"Lewis liked poker playing, and he was good. There was a big game of poker that went on in downtown Quiver, moving from basement to basement of the businesses and hotels. Only the best players in town were invited to the game, and it went on around the clock, moving from place to place all secretlike so nobody's wife would exactly know where her husband was any given night. Lewis and one other colored man were so good they were let into the game on Friday nights, when the miners got paid. Not exactly invited, but let in. My dad said Lewis probably fit in pretty well because he was so quick with a joke. Lewis lost some money, but not enough to make Belle very angry. Other Friday nights, he won some money, but not enough to buy her any modern conveniences, such as the wringer washer her heart desired. And then in the fall of 1920, he got on a lucky streak and won double his money three separate Friday nights in a row. It wasn't shrewd for a colored man to do that. Not in Quiver, Oklahoma, in 1920."

Celeste hesitated then and looked into the darkness for a while, chewing her lip. It was as though she was watching a scary movie in her head, trying to find a way to describe it. Then she began talking fast and using weird, nonsense language.

"One moonless night in late October, the Terrors crept secretly to their Klavern in the attic of Arvil Teschler's house. The Klaliff put the flag in its mount by the Sacred Altar, The Kloliff draped the Sacred Altar with the white satin Shield, and the Night-Hawk brought the fiery cross before the station of the Exalted Cyclops. The Kludd placed the Holy Bible on the shiny white altar drape, open to Romans twelve. Across the Bible he balanced a sharpened and polished sword. Then the other Terrors, robed and hooded, showing only their eyes, entered the Klavern from the outer dens where the sacred robes and vestments were stored. They solemnly took their positions in a double circle around the Altar, then all in the room pledged their allegiance to the Invisible Empire, and to the majesty and supremacy of the Divine Being. They swore together that they 'avowed the distinction between the races as has been decreed by the Creator.' They promised together 'to ever be true in the faithful maintenance of White Supremacy.' The Exalted Cyclops rose slowly from his throne in the corner and called out, 'My Terrors, what means the Fiery Cross?' And the others answered in loud voices, 'We serve and sacrifice for the right!' And then . . ."

When she didn't go on, I shook her shoulder. "Celeste," I hissed, "are you talking about your attic? All that stuff took place in your attic, back in the 1920's when Mr. Teschler's father owned the house?"

She turned in my direction, but she seemed to be looking right through me.

"The Exalted Cyclops and his Terrors came for Lewis that night, Frannie. They kicked in the front door. Belle jumped out of bed, and they slammed her against the wall with one of the lit torches they carried. She ran into the bedroom where the three children slept, and began hiding them as best she could, shoving them under the bed, stopping their mouths with the blanket so they wouldn't cry out. She saw the Terrors take Lewis by force, club him, yell at him to confess his crime of thievery, of cheating and plotting and using his wife's Louisiana Voodoo sorcery to take money from the pockets of hardworking white men. They drug him from the house, kicking him, spitting on him. Belle watched all this and didn't dare so much as scream.

"They took him to a secret cave and tortured him to death that night. When his friends followed his blood trail through the wilderness to retrieve his body the next day, he'd been so badly cut and burned they could barely recognize him. In her letters sent back to Louisiana, Belle wrote, 'I could not believe with these eyes of mine that it was my own dear Lewis.' "

Celeste slowly looked up at her manacled arm, then at mine.

"My great-grandfather died right here on this spot, Frannie! I know he did. It was the one piece missing from the puzzle. My father asked and asked, and some people said there used to be a cave around here somewhere but they couldn't remember where. Kelly knows the wilderness better than anyone. I should have known to ask her right off. Oh, Frannie, when I saw these manacles, I . . ."

She was suddenly trembling so hard that the chain attached to her left wrist rattled against the stone like chattering teeth. I stretched as far as I could to give her a one-armed hug, and when she rested her forehead on my shoulder I felt tears graze my arm.

A minute later she stood up, but grabbed my hand and clutched it hard.

"I'm not finished, Frannie. I need to tell you about the field.

"See, my great-grandfather wasn't the only person from Minetown tortured and killed back then. Not by a long shot. The upstairs windows at the Teschler house were always blacked out like they still are to this day, but everyone knew if there was light leaking from the edges of those dark windows, a meeting was going on and someone in Minetown was doomed to be dragged to his death later that night. It might be a colored man that had been heard talking against a white boss. It might be a man who'd looked at a white woman in an admiring way, or, that is, some white man had *reported* that was his look. Two Negro teenagers were dragged out of their mothers' houses, cut with knives, then drowned in the river for stealing two bottles of beer from a white store in Quiver. One of those boys' mothers clung to the long white robe of the Terror that was taking away her son. She got kicked in the face for her trouble. Her jaw was badly shattered, but the doctor at the mine infirmary refused to set it. He said he didn't have the skill, but everyone knew he was afraid to. Afraid of those white-robed, hooded Terrors with their lighted torches and hidden faces.

"Everyone was afraid. My dad says there were surely people in Quiver who wanted to help, but they must have thought it was too dangerous. When their consciences ached too bad, my dad said he figures they managed to convince themselves that the rash of deaths in Minetown were 'accidents,' or just 'one crazy colored man fighting another.'

"Then suddenly, when things were so hopeless, a new district judge was assigned to Quiver, and he was as brave as the old judge had been cowardly. Judge Howerton hadn't been in town six months before he did some investigating and issued warrants for the arrests of four white men suspected of being involved in twenty-some Minetown deaths."

There in the dark cave, I gave a quick, joyful jump that jerked my arm painfully backwards. "Yes!" I whispered. "Yes!"

"Frannie," Celeste warned with solemn sarcasm, "you might want to hold your applause till after I tell you what this all has to do with . . . the field."

She slowly shook her head.

"When Judge Howerton came to Quiver he brought a wife, a baby girl and a twelve-year-old son. The field was a lush green rectangle of old oak trees and prairie grass back then, and Judge Howerton bought it and had a big two-story house built on it for his family. There was one truly spectacular tree near the house—a spreading oak that my dad says had probably been growing for at least two hundred years. It was the judge's son's favorite place—Tad and his best friend James even built themselves a treehouse up there to hide out in. Frannie, we know all this because James . . . James was Lewis' oldest boy, ten years old when his father was killed and twelve when Tad Howerton came to town. James was my father's father."

I drew in a sharp breath and held it, waiting for her to go on.

"James and Tad were inseparable. Even as an old man, my Grandpa Chisholm talked about things they'd done together, mischievious things like dropping frogs down from that treehouse onto the heads of passersby, or sneaking whole pies from Tad Howerton's kitchen and eating themselves sick. The judge was disliked enough around town for his racial policies, and now his own son had a colored friend. But when Grandpa told us this part of the story, he always said, 'We knew we shouldn't of, but Tad and me, we just couldn't help running with each other.' Tad gave James a valuable fishing knife his own grandfather had given him, and James gave Tad his prized possession—the harmonica his father had owned."

Celeste closed her eyes, and lowered her voice to a whisper.

"Judge Howerton and his family were probably asleep when the hooded riders stormed that white house on a November midnight and set it on fire with torches. They galloped in a circle, hooting and yelling obscenities and thrusting their torches toward the judge and his wife and son as they stumbled out onto the lawn. The judge begged to be allowed to run back in to save his baby daughter, but instead four of those riders jumped from their horses to tie his hands and gag him, and by the light of that inferno they hanged him and his son Tad from that majestic oak tree. They were far too *civilized* and *God-fearing* to harm a white woman, so the judge's wife was spared to end her days up north, Dad thinks it was probably in Chicago.

"Frannie, the field smoldered for weeks. Folks in Quiver said it was because of all the seasoned wood used in that big, fine house, but folks in Minetown knew better. My great-grandmother wrote to her friends in Louisiana about the fire. I've got that letter memorized, Frannie. It's the kind of thing that sticks in your head. 'Everything on earth that blazes that hot is quickly burned out and extinguished, and new green grass grows up within a week,' my great-grandmother wrote. 'Only the devil's own work could burn so endless, feeding upon its bitter self till the skin of the very earth is forever scarred and blasted.'

"There was one thing left when that fire finally settled to cold ashes, and that was the flame-hardened black trunk of the big oak tree. That tree became the rallying place of the Terrors, even more than the attic room had been. It still had one scorched and jutting branch, and several Negro men were lynched from that branch over the next years. When they lynched someone, the Terrors set a wooden cross on fire beside the tree to draw attention to their handiwork. The lynchings only got worse after three of the Terrors were jailed for the deaths of the judge and his family.

"The night train from Kansas City to Tulsa went along the edge of Quiver back then, where the abandoned tracks still are, parallel with Route 66. You can almost see them from your patio if you know where to look."

I nodded silently. Celeste stopped and faced me, and her eyes were so sad and hurt and filled with questions that I couldn't breathe.

"I've thought about this a lot, Frannie. What do you think those night travelers would have thought when they glanced out their windows just in time to see a tall burning cross right next to a blasted tree with . . . with . . ."

She closed her eyes, shivering.

"What would they have *thought,* Frannie? And what would they have *felt?*"

CHAPTER 23

Celeste's father had found the key to our manacles hanging on its own special little hook inside one of the lockers in the awful upstairs room. He got us out of those terrible things lickety-split, then hugged Celeste tight. When she tried to talk, he shushed her and murmured, "I know, sweetheart. This has to be the place, all right. Shhhh. I know."

The two ranch hands that had come with Kelly's father rode Amelia and Heathcliff home while Celeste and Kelly and their fathers and I rode back to town in the Jeep.

It turned out *my* father had taken the boys somewhere, and Kelly hadn't been able to find him to bring him to the cave. That seemed like a huge lucky break, now. Both Celeste's and Kelly's fathers were way too quiet in the Jeep, and kept clenching and unclenching their jaw muscles. It was obvious Celeste and Kelly were

194

both in for the awful kind of after-hug lecture you got when you'd scared your dad witless.

When they let me off at my house, no one was home yet. I took a long shower, then paced around my room. I finally went to the kitchen and began making spaghetti, but my hands were shaking as I worked. I wanted to tear my brain out, smash things and howl.

Dad and the boys got home just as I was draining the noodles, and we ate. Mitch and Harley were all excited about the football scrimmage they'd been to at the high school, so they babbled on and on and I didn't have to say anything much.

"Where's your mother, Frannie?" Dad suddenly asked.

"I don't know," I murmured. "I figured you knew. Isn't she shopping or something?"

He shrugged. "I expected her home at noon, like she always is when she works Saturday morning. She probably did go out shopping." He winked at Harley. "Bet she got that new job and she's bringing us home some big gooey dessert to celebrate with."

Harley's eyebrows shot sky-high and he and Mitch licked their lips and rubbed their stomachs. I tried for a smile, but gave it up. Nobody was going to notice my mood anyway. Their minds were on football and gooey desserts.

Dad *did* notice, though. "Frannie, here's something that should cheer you up," he said. "They announced today that they're going to replace the lights and the bleachers clear around the stadium at the high school, to the tune of something like forty-thousand dollars. And they'll be donating the old lights and bleachers to Carver High, for their field, which has never had lights or permanent seating. So you see? This is what I've been trying to get across to you. The town really does go out of its way to keep things equal."

I looked down at my plate and wondered if the pressure building in my chest was going to explode my rib cage. Things began to throb at the edges, and I knew my days of worrying when I questioned his—this *town's*—viewpoint were over.

"What's equal about one school getting new stuff and the other one getting their leftover junk?" I asked fiercely, more fiercely than I ever thought I'd talk to either of my parents. I swallowed several times and pretended to concentrate on putting pepper on my spaghetti, though I hated pepper, and Dad knew it.

Suddenly, the kitchen door banged open and Mom stormed in. She threw her purse on the counter and kicked off her high heels so hard they sailed halfway across the room. She shoved herself backwards to slam the door closed, stomped to the sink, got a glass of water and threw it down her throat, then actually dropped the glass roughly back in the drainer like no one had even drunk from it.

We all just stared, forgetting to chew.

"Caroline?" Dad asked carefully. "Are you all right?"

She whirled around to face us and slumped back against the sink. "Mr. Joslen informed me that I was *far* too valuable as his personal secretary to be promoted to broker," she spat out, her eyes flashing. "I'd just be taking the job from a *man,* he said, and that just wouldn't be *right,* to deprive some working *man* of a job. Why did I want to waste my *assets* in some back office anyway, when it was important to have a *pretty little thing* to greet the customers up front? Then, he winked at me. He *winked* at me! I'm so good and tired of his winks I feel like . . . like just punching him right in the eye!"

Dad got up and started to walk toward her with his arms out, huglike. But she backed toward the stove, grabbed the ball of spaghetti noodles I'd left in a pan, and held them in front of her like a rubbery, jiggling weapon.

"Don't you *dare* be condescending to me, Sam!"

"You guys vamoose," I hissed to Mitch and Harley, and they slid out of their chairs and went skittering.

The phone rang. Mom stomped over to answer it, tossing the noodles back in the pan. "Hel-*lo!*" she demanded, stamping her bare foot for emphasis. Then her face instantly reddened and she put a hand to her forehead. "Oh, Mr. Chisholm! How nice to hear from you. I'm sorry about the way I answered the . . . what did you say? Well, no she hasn't told me about it, but maybe she's told her father."

I put my elbows on the table and my face in my hands. There was no way I could make a run for my room—Mom had instinctively moved across the doorway and blocked all escape with the phone cord.

After a few more short, polite phrases, Mom hung up the phone and stood looking from me to Dad and wiping the noodle slime from her hand onto her new green silk skirt.

"That was Mr. Chisholm, Sam. He . . . he invited us over tonight to see something he's got. An attic broom, I think he said. He said he's afraid we won't understand what the girls were up to this afternoon unless we see it for ourselves, this broom or whatever it is he's got. He's inviting Kelly and her parents, too. Frannie?"

I braced myself. "You're . . . you're ruining your skirt, Mom," I mumbled, helpfully.

"Frannie, were you *handcuffed* in a *cave* this afternoon?"

I gulped. "You know what? I'll bet he said *room,* not *broom* . . ." I began.

"The cave, Frannie," Dad interrupted solemnly. "Explain the *cave.*"

★   ★   ★

So I got the lecture, too, which I have to admit was only fair. It would probably have been much worse, but Dad had to stop to go ask Mrs. Castlehoff across the street to come and watch the boys.

And then, we drove over to the Chisholms' horrible house.

All eight of us walked slowly through the giant's awful shoebox that night. I clung to Dad's arm as Mr. Chisholm explained the Sacred Altar, the platform in the corner where the Exalted Cyclops sat, and the lockers with their ghostly robes and hoods. He even showed us a notary seal he'd found under a floorboard, a little silver machine that had been used to put the Terror's official mark on the death warrants of innocent people in Minetown.

"The Ku Klux Klan really flourished around here in the twenties and thirties, then slowly lost membership and dwindled in the forties," he told us. "I can find no real evidence of them still being a force around here in the fifties, though the last man to live here did organize secret monthly meetings in this room. Norman Teschler may have wanted to reignite the kind of fiery zeal the Klan had when his father, Arvil, lived here and was Grand Cyclops, but I can find nothing to indicate that he had any real success."

Daddy shook his head. "I knew old Norman was bitter and frustrated, but I never dreamed he was . . . crazy.

Thank God he wasn't the kind of man other men would follow, or all that might still be going on."

Mr. Chisholm folded his arms and frowned hard. We were all gathered around the table in the little outer room, the one with the shiny white cloth. I knew now that the creepy cross and crown design in the middle was the secret seal of the Ku Klux Klan.

"What are you thinking, Raymond?" Dad finally asked.

"Well, one way the Klansmen refer to themselves is as 'Patriots.' They would refer to you as an 'Alien,' Sam. You too, Jack. Now me? Me, they'd call me a 'Beast.'" He laughed a bitter laugh. "Theirs is a childishly mystical world of Patriots, Aliens and Beasts. If either of you men let it be known that you shared their philosophy, and if through elaborate interviewing and testing they found you trustworthy, they could 'naturalize' you through a secret initiation ceremony. Then you would achieve the status of Patriot, and be an official Klansman. And that naturalization ceremony can be so private that even other Klansmen don't know the identity of new initiates. In this day and age, you see, it wouldn't be socially acceptable to ride a rough horse through the streets, cursing and burning and lynching and thinking of yourself as a 'Terror.' In fact, it wouldn't even be socially acceptable to be led by someone as poorly thought of as Norman Teschler. No, these days the Klan seems to function most effectively as a support group, and has gone both 'legitimate' and underground to a greater degree than in the past. Mr. Joslen must have had some knowledge of the recent history of this place, since he saw fit to hurriedly seal up the attic before he tried to sell the house. But just because this room has been sealed doesn't mean there aren't other places in the area where Patriots get together, quite possibly robed so as to be incognito even to each other."

Kelly's father pushed back his Stetson and shook his head. "So, you're saying a good upstanding citizen of this town could be initiated in secret, and even his fellow ushers at church wouldn't be the wiser? He could get his regular fix of hatred with his anonymous Patriot friends, then do all kinds of secret mischief through his business and his connections in the community."

"I'm not saying it *is* happening here, I'm just saying it's happening in other places, and *could* be happening here. The kind of hatred that caused this room to be constructed in the first place isn't easily or quickly put aside."

At some point while Mr. Chisholm talked, I'd grabbed my wrist and begun squeezing it hard. I looked at Celeste, and she was doing the same thing, with the opposite wrist.

It was cold that night, but I opened my window anyway, propped my pillow on the sill, and settled in to stare sadly at the field. The moon was puffed-up orange and low in the sky, caught like an angry prisoner behind the bars of the rocket ship.

"Knock, knock," Dad said softly and gruffly, then opened my door.

I scooted enough to give him a place to sit on the edge of my bed.

"My two pretty girls are both mad at me at once. I guess I'm just too dumb to get with the twentieth century, huh?"

"Oh, Daddy." I turned to roll my eyes at him and couldn't keep from laughing. He had his mouth turned down and his hair was accidentally rumpled up, so he looked just like Harley and Mitch when they'd hurt themselves roughhousing in the yard.

"Think there's any hope for your poor old dad?"

I bounced to my knees and threw my arms around his neck. "Nah," I laughed. "No hope at all."

CHAPTER 24

On Sunday, Kelly and Celeste and I were more or less grounded. That is, none of us had the nerve to make plans with our parents' stony disapproval of our secret Saturday trail ride still hanging thickly in the air. But our fathers went somewhere together Sunday afternoon, almost like they were subbing for us. My dad took his toolbox, and Celeste told us Monday that her father had brought home the cave manacles wrapped in a horse blanket to add to his research materials.

On Monday, Celeste and I had tryouts again after school to narrow the seven Ladies of Harmony down to six. Carla sang better than I did. Miss Cantwell told us she'd post the results the next day, but I wistfully accepted the fact that my days in a select ensemble were over.

As it turned out, so were my mother's days as Mr. Joslen's secretary.

"She actually just up and *quit?*" Celeste looked impressed when I told her about it up in the starplace that night. "Quit a job she'd had for seven years?"

"Yeah. I should have known something was going to happen when she made star pancakes for breakfast again this morning. She told Mr. Joslen that he'd better rein in that winking stuff or his next secretary was liable to slap his face. And *then* she told him she might just go into business for herself and give him some real competition."

"All right, Mrs. Driscoll!" Celeste exclaimed, and we both hooted with appreciation.

So many times I've played that night up in the starplace over in my mind, because it was so typical. We giggled up there, we waved our arms around like fools, mimicking people at school and on TV. We let the wind run twisting fingers through our hair and brush little air kisses over our eyelids. We spontaneously sang a song together, maybe it was "Tammy's In Love" from the Debbie Reynolds movie we both liked, except for her boyfriend's hairstyle. And then we fell to our backs and looked at the stars and got quiet like they always made us get. We whispered about how the starlight we were seeing was thousands of years old. We whispered about whether we believed in UFO's, and whether God was up there among those stars or someplace more mysterious and hidden. Then we sat up and swished our hair around in the wind again and giggled and talked a little longer about things like whether Jay should come back and marry Charlotte. Maybe we stood up and practiced the peppermint twist. Maybe we split an Almond Joy or an Orange Crush.

People want to know the future, but life would never be perfect if that could happen.

That typical night up in our starplace was perfect because I didn't have the slightest inkling it would be our last.

At the end of choir the next day, Miss Cantwell posted a list of the girls in the Ladies of Harmony, just tacked it quickly onto the bulletin board and slipped into her office.

Carla had replaced Celeste.

"There . . . has to be a mistake!" I whispered, thunderstruck. "She meant to put Carla in my spot, not yours! Come on, let's go tell her what she did."

"Let it drop, Frannie," Celeste said quietly over my shoulder.

I whirled to face her. "Let it *drop?* What are you *talking* about? She made a simple mistake, Celeste! She was probably thinking about something else and just copied the name down wrong!"

She shook her head. "You still don't get it, do you?"

Her voice was flat, and her eyes were cold.

"Let's go *ask* her, Celeste! Come *on!*" I grabbed her arm.

"Let me *go,* Frannie!" She shook off my hand and stepped angrily back, then stood glaring at me. "Didn't you learn at the bowling alley that there are huge gaps in your understanding of what it's like to be me? I'm not going to have you holding on to me again while another white person humiliates me in public! I *said* let it drop, so let it drop!"

She turned and disappeared.

The world went spinning away from me. Where was I, who was I? My blood was beating in my ears, and my skin was on fire.

From miles away I heard the tiny click of Miss Cantwell's door opening, and then her face loomed in front of me.

"Frannie, I'm counting on you to make Celeste understand that this is by no means anything personal, okay? We just needed a lighter voice to balance with Carla's, since she's still recovering from her illness and not singing out very strongly. Celeste has an absolutely beautiful voice, just a bit overwhelming for this particular mix."

Her three-sentence speech sounded logical and compassionate. Later, when I could think straighter, I realized that was because it had been well rehearsed.

I kept swallowing and swallowing, but my throat wouldn't work. *You've got to think about the blend,* Tricia's self-righteous voice kept saying in my head. *The blend, the blend, the blend.*

I had to get out of there. Something was weighing down my arms, keeping me from escaping. I looked down at my books, couldn't figure out just exactly what they were, dropped them into Miss Cantwell's wide metal trash can, and ran.

First, out of the school. Then, to my house, to my room. I smashed the big turquoise pig with the yellow daisies that held my life savings—somewhere around twenty-three dollars. I dropped to my knees and filled my sweater pockets with those quarters and pennies and some shards of turquoise glass I couldn't take the time to separate out from the money.

I loped through the field with my ankles twisting and my pockets slapping painfully against my thighs. I ran straight onto Highway 66. Straddling the yellow center line, I stuck out my thumb. A couple of cars swerved to avoid me and the drivers gestured so violently that their anger got through my fog and I remembered you were supposed to hitchhike from the side of the road, not the middle of it.

I ran back to the side of the road, but this time when I tried to stick out my thumb my hands came up to cover my face instead, and when I discovered that my face was already slick with tears, I sat down in the litter-studded ditch and sobbed and sobbed.

When those businessmen at the Chamber of Commerce banquet voted us the three-hundred dollars, did they know they would easily push Celeste out? Or did the mothers decide to do that when they were looking through that fancy dress catalog, dreaming how their creamy-white daughters would look in five-hundred-dollar dresses? When did they tempt Miss Cantwell with the dresses and make *her* knuckle under to their plan? Miss Cantwell didn't need a lighter voice. If she wanted those dresses, she needed a lighter *skin.*

I rocked side to side, sick to my stomach. I couldn't run away from my parents and family, and I couldn't stay in this town.

Finally, I slouched back through the field and climbed up into the rocket. I sat there for hours, willing Celeste to come.

Rain started falling, a light rain that would turn to a downpour overnight then settle into a misty gloom for the rest of the week. "Come on, Celeste," I whispered to the distance, but the only answering sound was the soggy snap of field weeds breaking beneath the pressure of the rain.

I'd listed to my side and fallen asleep up there when she finally came.

"Frannie! You're gonna wind up with double pneumonia, girl."

I jerked up, disoriented. She was adjusting an umbrella so it covered us both. I shoved wet hair off my face, shivering. "What *took* you so long?"

"Dad and I were talking, making plans. I called you, but your little brother said he couldn't find you. I'm sorry, Frannie. I didn't mean to lash out like that at school. I just get so frustrated I can hardly see straight sometimes."

"I thought it all through, Celeste, and I know what happened. The parents of some of those girls made Miss Cantwell do it, and she was too wimpy to resist. It had absolutely nothing to do with your singing."

She shrugged, and I knew then that that had been immediately obvious to her.

"However it happened, it doesn't matter now," she said.

Now. "Stop it!" I yelled, pushing my hands over my ears, muting her voice with my soaked hair. "Don't say another word! If you say another word I'll never, ever speak to you again!

"We're leaving," she said quietly. "Day after tomorrow."

I angrily batted her umbrella away from me, then staggered to my feet on the slick, wet wood. "You knew, even in the cave!" I spat out. "You said it was the only chance you might get to tell me the story of your grandfather. You . . . knew, and you just let me go on thinking, thinking . . ."

"I *suspected,*" she said, looking up into my face. "I suspected I'd be cut from the double trio, and I was, Frannie."

She pulled at the cuff of my sock, and I resisted for a while, then sank back down, pressing my back against the bars across from her. I'd never felt such red-hot fury.

"What about . . . what about *me?*" I demanded. "Is that miserable little ensemble so important to you that you'd . . . you'd just throw away . . . throw away everything . . ."

My voice broke. For a while we both just sat there, not looking at each other.

Then she said, "Frannie, my parents gave me my choice of coming here this year or staying in St. Louis, but I could tell they sort of thought I could learn things from . . . from a place like this. Things about my history. Things about . . . people, mostly."

I longed to ask her exactly what she meant by that, but I was just too angry. She'd learned lots of awful things about people in Quiver, that was for sure. But hadn't she learned anything from me, and from the other people in my crowd? Her crowd, now?

"But I'm discovering just how much I *need* my music, maybe because it's been so, well, hard," she continued softly. "If I'm not going to be allowed to be in anything challenging here, I don't want to lose the precious time and momentum I could have back in St. Louis, making progress. Dad's research is complete, and we both miss Mom."

Still I didn't look at her.

"Try and understand, Frannie," she finished. "I've

made a huge decision. I'm going to try to really excel in music, that one thing. And I've got to get started."

I put my elbows on my knees and my face in my hands. I felt her pull on my sleeve and I yanked my arm to my chest and shoved around so my back was to her.

"Frannie, I have something to show you," she said.

"I don't want to see it," I informed her bitterly, gulping back tears. "Just leave me alone. Go home and *pack!*"

She reached around me and dropped something in my lap.

It was the burned and blackened harmonica. My chest heaved and ached so much I thought I'd die.

"We think this was in Tad's pocket when he was hanged that night, Frannie." Celeste's voice was full of tears, too. "We think it was dropped and left to be burned again and again."

I banged my forehead with both fists.

"Frannie, I know you're thinking you'll quit the ensemble, but you can't do that, because you know who they'd blame."

I scrubbed my wet face hard with my sweatered fists, then clenched the precious piece of charred wood and metal and spun around to hug her.

"I couldn't help running with you, Celeste," I whispered, sobbing into her hair.

"Oh, star sister, I couldn't help running with you, either."

EPILOGUE

Somewhere over the Midwest, 1986 . . .

I can usually concentrate when I'm on a dark jet filled with sleeping people, just me and my notebook meeting a midnight deadline for my paper, *The St. Louis Post Dispatch.* But ten minutes ago I glanced out the small window at my shoulder and the clouds parted just long enough for me to see something unexpected on the ground far below. It was a cross, made of lights. I'm sure some church laid it out purposely, installed all those halogen bulbs along several city blocks to bring some kind of peace and comfort to weary sky travellers.

But to this traveller on this night, it brought a flood of memories instead.

The college girl in the seat next to me is asleep. She told me about the boyfriend she's been with in Cincinnati this weekend, and I suspect she's dreaming about him now. A few minutes ago, she complimented me on the rhinestone-studded bobby pin in my hair, told me she just loved "retro." Retro! How can twenty-five years have passed so quickly?

Twenty-five years since Celeste left that cold, rainy November weekend and Mr. Chisholm did my mother the honor of asking her to sell his house in Quiver. Twenty-five years since my parents took apart the giant's shoebox and turned the attic into living space, then sold the old Teschler house at such a profit that Mom's commission helped her get set up in her own real estate office.

Twenty-five years since the Ladies of Harmony took a beating at the showchoir competition. A group from Tulsa won, and there was grumbling for months around Quiver that it was because there were three black judges among the nine and that two of the girls in the winning group were black and one was "Polynesian or Korean or something." Celeste and I had a big laugh over that when I went to visit her in St. Louis that Christmas.

None of us—not one of our group—hung around Quiver after high school graduation. In fact, we scrambled out of there like we were being chased. After Celeste, we all understood deep in our bones that if a place refuses to be a launch pad for one person, it can't function as a launch pad for anyone.

I go back to visit, though, because my parents are still there. Mom is still fighting the "equal housing" fight, and now Mitch has a new law degree and helps her. They say it's still an uphill battle all the way. I wonder once in a while about all those endless people passing through Quiver on Route 66. Do they look up from their magazines or video games long enough to notice an iron rocket still trying unsuccessfully to rise from a blighted, trash-studded field? What do they think about that? What do they feel?

Well, I guess we're all night travellers on this rickety starship, Earth. The things we see out our small, clouded windows sometimes shock us, and often puzzle us, but they're usually left quickly behind as we rush headlong toward tomorrow. Usually, but not always.

To *work,* Fran!

DIVA SHINES AS NILE PRINCESS
by Francine Driscoll, staff writer

Ms. Celeste Chisholm, coloratura soprano and one-time resident of our city of St. Louis, dazzled opera lovers at Cincinnati's historic Music Hall tonight in a sold-out performance of Verdi's masterpiece, Aida. *Upon her third curtain call, Chisholm thrilled the audience with the opening-night gesture she reserves for appearances here in the Midwest, blowing kisses and throwing flowers back to the crowd . . .*

And then she always touches her own "retro" bobby pin, and whether I'm there in her audience or only with her in my thoughts, I feel that interstellar connection and touch back, sending pride and love.